"I'll have the steak, please," said Hunter

"How would you like it cooked?" Gussie asked.

"Rare," he said. Of course.

"With raw blood," Gussie said, as if to herself, scribbling down the order. "Would you like a knife and fork, or would you prefer to tear at it with your teeth?"

Hunter met her look appreciatively. "A knife and fork, please. I'm feeling civilized tonight...."

Jessica Hart had had a haphazard career before she began writing for Harlequin Romance. Her experience ranged from a waitress, theater production assistant, and outback cook, to news-desk secretary and English teacher. She has worked her way around the world from Egypt, Kenya, Jakarta and Australia. She now lives in the North of England, where she is studying for a degree in history.

Books by Jessica Hart

HARLEQUIN ROMANCE
3213—THE TROUBLE WITH LOVE
3231—WOMAN AT WILLAGONG CREEK
3302—THE BECKONING FLAME
3334—A SENSIBLE WIFE

DEFIANT LOVE
Jessica Hart

Harlequin Books

TORONTO • NEW YORK • LONDON
AMSTERDAM • PARIS • SYDNEY • HAMBURG
STOCKHOLM • ATHENS • TOKYO • MILAN
MADRID • WARSAW • BUDAPEST • AUCKLAND

ISBN 0-373-17239-7

DEFIANT LOVE

Copyright © 1993 by Jessica Hart.

First North American Publication 1995.

CHAPTER ONE

'HERE they come.'

Gussie wriggled forward and peered through the bracken. A sleek black car, the kind that looked as if it might snarl if you went too close, was just drawing up by the gate to the field, and as she watched a man got out and closed the door behind him. He was powerfully built, with dark hair and an angular face, and she had a fleeting impression of charismatic authority before he turned away.

He walked over to the gate and stood with his hands in his pockets, studying the view. It was a peaceful scene. Black thunderclouds were gathering menacingly behind the hills, but the golden evening light still shafted defiantly down on to the meadow which rolled gently down to the river.

The man seemed unaware of the group hidden on the edge of the oak wood behind him. Lost in thought, he let his gaze rest on the long grass, its luxuriant green interspersed with tiny stitchwort and splashy red poppies.

Probably working out how long it would take him to plough it all up and cover it with concrete, Gussie thought bitterly, waving the flies out of her eyes.

'That must be Hunter Scott,' she whispered. Janet, their contact in the estate agency, had tipped them off that the London developer would be coming up for another look at the site, and it seemed she had been right.

She had told Gussie that the estate agent would be with him, but there was no sign of anyone else. 'He must have decided to come on his own after all.'

'So much the better.' Mark crouched down beside her and regarded Hunter Scott with a sneer. 'He's going to get a shock when he finds himself surrounded!'

'Ye-es,' Gussie agreed doubtfully. Her clear golden-brown eyes rested on the man standing still and thoughtful by the gate. From her hiding place, she could see little of him other than the well-cut hair and the broad shoulders beneath the tweed jacket, but there was just something in the way he stood that suggested a man unlikely to be easily shocked or surprised.

Hunter was a good name for him, she thought. There was a watchful air about him, a suggestion of controlled strength in his stance.

Mark misunderstood her hesitation. 'Don't tell me you've lost your nerve now we've got this far!' he whispered in disgust. 'I told Simon you weren't tough enough to lead this protest!'

Gussie flushed. 'Of course I haven't!' she hissed back.

It was true that Simon had been doubtful about putting her in command, but she had begged for the chance to prove that she was as committed as everyone else at Future Green. They all thought that because she wasn't loud and aggressive about her beliefs she didn't really care, but she did. She cared desperately about the countryside, too much to be content with her present contribution of collecting signatures for petitions. Gussie wanted to show that she was capable of real action. Saving Whin Farm from the developers was her big opportunity to show that she wouldn't shrink from a fight if it was necessary.

Unconsciously, she squared her shoulders and beckoned the group forward. There were nine of them altogether, all young, all dressed alike in jeans and dark green T-shirts with Future Green's bold logo across their chests.

'Are you all ready?' she asked in a low voice. She had never led a protest before, and she had vague thoughts of making a stirring speech, but it was hard when you had to whisper and the flies buzzed excitedly around her eyes. The sooner they could get out of this bracken the better.

'Remember, we just want to give him a fright, and let him know that we won't let him get away with his plans for Whin Farm. These companies hate any publicity, so I rang the *Echo* and asked them to send a photographer along to witness the first shot in our campaign, as it were. His investors are bound to take fright when they hear how serious the opposition is.'

There were several nods of approval at this, and Gussie felt insensibly cheered as she glanced at her watch. 'I can't see any sign of the photographer, though,' she had to admit. 'What do you all think? Shall we wait for him to turn up, or shall we tackle Hunter Scott while he's on his own?' Future Green was committed to a truly democratic approach.

'Let's get on with it,' Mark said impatiently. 'We can't hang around here all evening, and for all we know you might have given the photographer the wrong instructions!'

Gussie struggled to subdue her resentment. Her quietness and deceptively fragile appearance hid a burning passion for nature that was rarely suspected by those who had never witnessed her temper roused in defence of an ill-treated animal or in fury at a despoiled piece of countryside. Friends and family pointed out that most people found such hot-headed passion laughable or embarrassing. It was far more effective to use cool, well-reasoned arguments, they said, and Gussie tried very hard to follow their advice, but being cool never seemed to get her very far. She had joined Future Green a few months ago, hoping that here at least she would find some kindred spirits who felt as passionately about the environment as she did, but somehow she had never seemed to fit in with the group. Gussie suspected it was because she wasn't interested in their interminable discussions about politics, but surely it was more important to be out *doing* something for the environment instead of sitting around talking about it?

Still, this was her chance to act instead of listen. She mustn't let Mark intimidate her. She must be cool, decisive, a leader.

Shooting a worried look at the storm clouds, Gussie made up her mind. All the signs were that they were in for a thunderstorm. It might freshen the air, which was uncomfortably hot and close, but if she hesitated too long their protest would be washed out altogether. She took a deep breath. 'All right,' she said. 'Let's go. Remember, we're all fighting for a green future!'

At her signal, the group erupted into yells as they burst from the undergrowth, and ran towards Hunter Scott, brandishing placards and shouting defiance.

Infuriatingly, Hunter didn't appear the least bit intimidated to find himself suddenly surrounded by nine fierce
protestors, and Gussie began to feel a little ridiculous.
It was all very well making a lot of noise and waving
placards, but their vehemence seemed rather unnecessary when faced with one calm man who merely
raised an interrogative eyebrow and waited.

Signalling to the others to quieten down, she stepped
forward.

'Mr Scott?'

'Yes?' He showed no surprise that she knew his name.
He had a strong face, Gussie saw, with a forceful nose
and chin and amused, intelligent eyes the blue-grey
colour of slate. As her gaze met his, she stepped back
involuntarily, unprepared for the full impact of his personality. There was a compelling quality about him, a
carefully leashed power that the glinting laughter in his
eyes did nothing to disguise. This man was tough, Gussie
realised with a small shock, and she shifted uncomfortably as he took a silent inventory of her.

She was coltishly slender, and her gentle face was given
character by a pair of striking eyes beneath winged dark
brows. Framed by naturally dark lashes that emphasised
the unusual colour, they were a clear honey-brown
flecked with amber and old gold. Her thick, coppery
hair was tied back in a ponytail, but the severe look she
had hoped to achieve was rather spoiled by the wisps
that kept falling about her face.

The amusement in Hunter Scott's expression deepened
as he studied her, and for some reason Gussie felt the
blood rush to her cheeks. Out of the corner of her eye
she could see Mark shaking his head at her courteous

tone, and although it didn't come naturally she forced herself to sound more truculent.

'Mr Scott, we represent Future Green, and I have been chosen as spokesperson this evening. Future Green is an environmental pressure group, and, although we are naturally concerned with the future of the earth as a whole, our particular responsibility is the area around Bracklewick.'

She knew that instead of the assertive effect she had aimed for she had sounded merely pompous and stilted, and it was obvious that Hunter Scott thought so too.

'And you've taken time off from saving the world to come and see me?' he mocked. 'I'm flattered!'

'You might be less flattered when you hear what we have to say,' she said, eyeing him with hostility. He was a typical bloated developer, grown soft on profits, sneering and jeering at anyone prepared to stand up and fight to protect the countryside!

'And what exactly is that?' Hunter asked with deceptive softness, but the gleaming amusement had vanished from his eyes, leaving them sharp and unnervingly hard. They seemed to bore through Gussie, who rapidly revised her opinion. There was nothing soft or bloated about this man. Suddenly, he looked alarmingly tough, and for one craven moment she wished that she had never asked to lead the protest against him, before the thought of what he was planning to do to Whin Farm squared her shoulders and stiffened her spine.

'We know all about your plans for Whin Farm,' she said, hoping that she sounded braver than she felt. 'And we're here to tell you that you'd better abandon them right now, because we don't intend to let you develop in this area.'

There was an encouraging murmur of support from the group behind her and she lifted her chin to meet Hunter's eyes defiantly, but he was not noticeably impressed.

'Don't you think you're exceeding your so-called responsibility somewhat?' he said coldly. 'I hate to point it out, but Whin Farm belongs to Mr Wilson. If he chooses to sell his land to me, that's his business, not yours.'

'Anything that affects the countryside around Bracklewick is our business,' Gussie said, gaining confidence. 'The environment belongs to all of us and we're not prepared to stand by and let you destroy it. Whin Farm isn't going to be another casualty of development!' Where was the photographer from the *Echo*? she wondered crossly. He should have been here to record this confrontation! Surely this was a bigger story than the fêtes and jumble sales that usually filled the front page of the *Echo*?

Hunter sighed. 'Why on earth would I want to destroy the environment?' he asked.

'To make money!' Gussie flashed back, annoyed by his lack of concern at her accusations and more than a little ruffled by the mocking gleam that had reappeared in his slate-coloured eyes. Did she have a smut on her nose or something? That cold look had been unnerving enough, but somehow the glint of amusement was even more unsettling. Something about him set her on edge; she wished he would decide whether he was going to be furious or entertained.

'Making money is certainly one of my interests,' Hunter admitted without embarrassment. 'It would be foolish to pretend otherwise, but it's not the only one. I've also got an interest in preserving the environment as far as possible, and while your concern is commendable,' he added with dismissive sarcasm, 'I'm afraid it's misplaced. I can assure you that you've no need to worry about my plans for Whin Farm.'

'No need to worry?' Gussie echoed incredulously. He didn't really think she would believe *that*, did he? 'No need to worry when you're about to turn Whin Farm into a leisure centre?'

She waved an arm at the woodlands behind her. 'You don't care about what happens to the wildlife when you cut down those trees! You don't care that the meadow you've been eyeing so greedily is home to nearly thirty species of wild flowers! Oh, no, what do they matter when you can turn them into car parks and make lots of money? It makes me sick the way you people tear up chunks of the countryside in the name of progress and then tell us not to worry about it!'

Her golden eyes flashed. It was impossible to remember all those resolutions about cool, reasoned arguments when her blood was boiling with fury at his dismissive attitude. 'Groups like Future Green are a joke to you, aren't they? You sneer at us, but this is one occasion when you're going to have to take us seriously!'

Hunter Scott looked at her. 'I might take you more seriously if you bothered to do a bit of research before jumping to conclusions,' he said in a cutting voice. 'I'm not going to cut down the woods, and nor am I going to turn the meadow into a car park. If you'd seen the plans, as you claim to have done, you would know that. As it is, I'd respectfully suggest that you don't know what you're talking about!'

'You don't deny that you're going to build a leisure centre, though?' Gussie accused, refusing to let him push her on to the defensive.

'No, I don't deny that,' he said with exaggerated patience. 'There's no secret about it, and I've already got planning permission. Frankly, I can't see any reason for you to make this fuss. Mr Wilson is happy to sell to us, and that's surely his decision?'

'Of course he's happy to sell!' Gussie cried. 'It doesn't mean that he approves of what you're going to do with his farm! He's been wanting to retire since his wife died, but nobody's been interested in buying a run-down farm like this. I'm not surprised that he jumped at any offer!'

Hunter put his hands in his pockets. He was relaxed, apparently unperturbed by her hostility, but there was a hard edge to his voice. 'Hasn't it occurred to you that if you succeed in preventing this deal going through— admittedly a very unlikely outcome!—you'll destroy Mr Wilson's future too? Or do people not matter to you as much as your fine words?'

The treacherous colour was creeping up Gussie's cheeks again. She knew she was on shaky ground on this point, but Simon had reassured her that they were right. 'Of course they do,' she said. 'But what happens to the environment affects all of us.'

'I'm sure that'll be a great comfort to Mr Wilson if his sale falls through,' he said caustically. 'What about all the jobs that the project will provide? Have you thought about the people who might like a chance of employment in the country, or are they not worth taking into account either?'

'People can argue for themselves.' Gussie was beginning to sound less sure of herself and she searched around frantically for something to support her argument. 'There's a badger's set on the farm. Who's going to talk for them?'

Hunter gave an exasperated sigh. 'Are you seriously asking me to go to my backers and tell them that we can't build at Whin Farm because we might disturb a few badgers?'

'Yes,' Gussie muttered. Why did people always make you feel so ridiculous when you stood up for animals?

'I can't help feeling that if you had as much concern for people as you do for animals you might have a more effective argument,' Hunter pointed out acidly and Gussie bit her lip.

Raking his fingers through his hair, he looked at her, taking in the stubborn tilt of her chin and the mute appeal in her topaz eyes. 'Look,' he went on more gently, 'I'm not going to hurt the badgers or anything else. I really think you should find out the full facts before you take your protests any further. I suspect you'll find that you're making a mountain out of a molehill.'

Taken unawares by his abrupt change of tone, Gussie stared at him. His expression was faintly exasperated, but the grey-blue eyes were steady and she wanted desperately to believe him.

Before she could think of what to say, Mark had shouldered past her, impatient of her lack of aggression. 'I'm not fooled by all this talk, even if Gus is!' he sneered and grabbed hold of Hunter's arm to swing him round.

'We know exactly what you're up to! You're just a typical reactionary! You think the land's yours to do what you want with, but it's not like that any more. You and your kind have corrupted the environment for long enough, and now we're fighting back!'

Gussie's face was burning with humiliation. Mark had no business taking over and not bothering to conceal his contempt for her attempts to reason with Hunter. But perhaps he was right. She *had* been perilously close to trusting him, and this was too important an issue to let herself be taken in by the deceptively reassuring light in a pair of eyes.

She saw Hunter glance at her, and then down at Mark's hand on his arm. Then he looked Mark square in the eyes. He didn't say a word, but Mark dropped his hand abruptly and stepped back.

'Why don't you grow up?' he said to Mark in a scathingly quiet voice that was somehow more frightening than a shout. 'If you're that concerned, go out and deal with some of the real problems that face the world. Do something useful instead of wasting your time and mine with childish objections to a scheme that will do more for the community and the environment than all your demonstrations ever will.'

'We won't be wasting our time if we stop you building on Whin Farm!' Mark blustered. 'You'd better watch out! We won't rest until we see you go running back to London with your tail between your legs!' As if aware that his threats sounded unconvincing, he turned his back on Hunter. 'Come on, let's go!' he said to the others, and strode off down the road, holding his placard aggressively before him.

One or two of them glanced hesitantly at Gussie before shrugging and trailing after him. There was no point in hanging around here.

Gussie had no choice but to follow. A fine leader she had been! She had made a mess of the whole thing, she realised disconsolately. Biting her lip, she turned to go after them, only to find that Hunter was watching her.

Their eyes held. Expecting triumph, she was surprised to see what might have been compassion in his eyes, along with that disquieting gleam of amusement as if he found them all silly and childish. The idea was galling. Immediately, her chin went up, pride coming to her rescue. He might dismiss them now, but they would show him!

Shooting him a defiant look, she turned on her heel and marched after Mark and the rest of the group.

She caught up with them as they rounded a bend in the road. She glanced over her shoulder once before they went out of sight, hoping that Hunter Scott would be staring after them in consternation, but he was leaning on the gate as if he had already forgotten them.

'Well, that wasn't much of a success, was it?' said Mark as Gussie came up. 'He ran rings round you, Gus! You were ready to believe everything he said!'

'There's no harm in listening to what he has to say, surely?' she tried to excuse herself, uncomfortably aware of how tempting it had seemed simply to trust Hunter Scott as he had asked.

Mark snorted. 'Wise up, Gus! You don't think a man like that's got anything to say worth listening to, do you? No, when I tell Simon what happened, I think he'll agree that we need an altogether tougher approach on this one.'

Without giving Gussie a chance to reply, he walked over to the battered old car that was parked in a gateway. 'Who wants a lift back to town?' he asked, tossing the car keys in his hand. 'Come on, we can squeeze everyone in!' Feeling that he had made his point, Mark evidently felt that he could afford to be generous. 'What about you, Gus?'

'It's all right, thank you,' she said a little stiffly. 'I'm on my bike.'

She secretly disapproved of the fact that both Mark and Simon had cars, even if they were old and battered. They were supposed to be encouraging people to cycle or use public transport, and Gussie thought it was important to practise what they preached. But when she had tentatively raised the point with Simon, he had explained to her at length just why he was justified in driving around Bracklewick.

'Sometimes the end justifies the means, Gus,' he had said, and Gussie had nodded, although afterwards she couldn't quite remember what he had said to convince her.

She was very impressed by Simon. He had curly hair and intense green eyes, and, more important, he was the prime mover in Future Green. It wouldn't be too much to say that it was his group, she thought, knowing that nothing would ever get done without his inspiration. At one point he had worked for one of the big environmental pressure groups in London, and she admired the fact that he had given it all up to come back to Bracklewick and set up Future Green. 'It's what happens at grass roots that really counts,' he was fond of saying.

Gussie watched Mark's car out of sight, and then began to walk slowly along the lane to where she had left her bike beneath the hedgerow. Pulling off her hair-band, she shook her hair free so that it tumbled about her face. It would be wonderful to be like Simon and know exactly what you wanted to do. Since she had left college, she had been trying to decide on a career, but she had soon found that she was not alone in wanting a job where she could have a real impact on the future of the planet. She had applied to all the environmental charities and pressure groups, but they only wanted people with relevant experience. All Gussie had was a burning desire to save the countryside she loved so much.

In the end, she had come home deciding that she would have to gain the much quoted experience by working as a volunteer, and she had thrown herself whole-heartedly into Future Green's activities. Working in a local wine bar earned her just enough money to support herself, and, although Simon thought it was strange, she was quite happy living with her family again. Her parents were warm and loving, and it was cheaper, even if it *was* less trendy. Sometimes Gussie forgot that it was sup-posed to be a temporary arrangement until she had gained enough experience to get a proper job, and there were times, too, when she wondered just how happy she would be away from Northumberland. The kind of jobs she could apply for at first were all based in big cities, and it would be a wrench to leave the moors with their wide skies, and the gentler wooded valleys where the oaks leant across the streams.

Every season had its own enchantment. Gussie could never decide which she preferred. In winter, the sky was

a gun-metal-grey and the garden birds fluffed up their
feathers against the cold. There were days when the frost
glittered and the bare trees stood out in stark silhouette
against the diamond-bright air, and the cold set her teeth
on edge. Every spring seemed more beautiful than the
last with verges awash with wild flowers and the larches
decked out in fresh, lacy green, and in May Gussie would
decide that it was definitely her favourite time of year.
She had always changed her mind by autumn, though.
She loved the faint appley smell on the air and the way
the gusty wind blew the fallen leaves around in a tum-
bling blur of gold and copper and rust.

It was early June now and the countryside was trembling on the edge of summer. Gussie's steps slowed and
she plucked at a piece of long grass to chew as she contemplated the view. Fat cows browsed knee-deep in the
lush summer grass and the sheep on the far side of the
river were neat white splodges against the green. The
hills rose behind them, their usual savannah-brown gilded
with gold as the late afternoon sunshine slanted down
like a biblical picture.

This was the land Hunter Scott wanted to develop.
Gussie frowned and threw down the piece of grass. She
had made no impression on him at all. It was hard to
know what to make of him. She shivered slightly, remembering how his eyes had changed from gleaming
amusement to steely inflexibility. He would be a formidable adversary, she thought. Mark could say what
he liked, but she didn't think he would get anywhere by
threatening Hunter Scott.

Still thinking about Hunter, Gussie rested her eyes on
the far hills, but as she watched the light disappeared,

as abruptly as if someone had thrown a switch. She glanced up and saw that the heavy black clouds had rolled over the sun. The first warning raindrop splattered on her hand and she grimaced. It was a long ride home and it looked as if it was going to be a very wet one.

She had better get moving. Bending down to retrieve her bike, she lifted it up carefully so as not to disturb too many plants and set it on the road. The rain was gathering momentum and in the distance there was an ominous rumble. She wished she had thought to bring a jacket with her, but it had been such a lovely day when she had set out that there had seemed little point. She should have remembered how quickly the weather could change! A light might have been a good idea, too, she realised. The thunder clouds were so low that it was as dark as a November afternoon.

It was at that point that Gussie realised that the chain had come off the bike. She bent and looked at it in dismay. It had been loose for some time, and she had meant to get it tightened, but she had been late leaving the restaurant and in a hurry to make the agreed rendezvous with the group.

Well, it wasn't the end of the world. She had fixed it before. It just meant that she was going to get wet before she had even started. With a sigh, Gussie turned the bike upside-down and rested it on its saddle and handlebars. It didn't seem to be her day.

The rain ran down her neck as she crouched down beside the bike and tried to loop the chain back on to its cogs. It was infuriating the way it seemed just too short to fit, and she remembered that she had always used a screwdriver to lever the last bit on before.

She persevered, but her hands were soon black with oil and her face red with exertion. Sitting back on her heels for a rest, she pushed the hair out of her eyes in frustration, leaving an oily smudge on her cheek. She would never get home at this rate.

It was pelting down now, and she was cold in her thin T-shirt. The gloomy light made it hard to see what she was doing, and she longed to be back in the warm and dry.

Gussie blinked the rain out of her eyes, and applied herself to the chain with renewed energy, muttering and cursing under her breath as it refused to co-operate. Intent on her efforts and deafened by the rain, she was unaware of the approaching vehicle until she saw light reflecting off the metal frame of the bike.

Looking up, she froze in horror as she saw the car bearing inexorably down on her. She had often seen rabbits mesmerised by headlights and wondered why they didn't move, but now she knew exactly how they felt. As if in slow motion, she managed to scramble to her feet, but there was no more time to escape. Gussie squeezed her eyes tight and held out her arms in futile attempt to ward off the car before it hit her.

Time seemed to stand still as she waited for the collision, but at the very last moment there was a scream of brakes on protesting tyres. The sound seemed to fill the air, drowning out even the rain, and then suddenly it stopped, leaving an echoing, unnatural silence in its wake.

CHAPTER TWO

A DOOR slammed. Quick footsteps, and then a hard hand grasped her arm.

'Are you all right? Did I hit you?'

Gussie opened her eyes. Hunter Scott was looking down at her with urgent concern, and the sheer impact of his personality jolted her back to reality. It was as if he had twice the wattage of ordinary men, and she could feel his strength reviving her, surging through her from the touch of his hand.

His grip tightened as she said nothing, just stared at him with eyes that were dark and wide with shock.

'You're not hurt, are you?'

Slowly she shook her head. 'N-no.'

'I thought I'd hit you,' he said, and for the first time she realised that he was as shaken as she was. Reaction sharpened his voice at the near-miss. 'I suppose you realise you could have been killed sitting in the middle of the road like that, you little idiot! I didn't see you until I was practically on top of you.'

'Nothing ever comes along this road,' Gussie said, warmed by an invigorating flicker of anger at his accusations. *She* wasn't the one who had been racing along the road! 'And if it does, it drives at a sensible speed!'

'I was driving at a perfectly safe speed,' he snapped. 'I could hardly have expected to find someone sitting in the middle of the road in the rain, wearing dark clothes that make her practically invisible! Did you *want* to get run over?'

'Of course not!' Gussie was still buoyed up by an anger that was mostly a reaction to the sheer terror of the car heading straight for her. She didn't want to think that she probably had Hunter Scott's driving skill to thank for the fact that she wasn't badly hurt.

'Then what *were* you doing?'

'I was mending my bike,' she said sulkily as her anger began to fade into a guilty realisation that she had been partly at fault.

'Was it necessary to do it right in the middle of the road?' he enquired sarcastically, and Gussie was glad that her flush was disguised by the murky light.

'I've told you, nothing comes along here.'

'I've come along,' Hunter pointed out.

'Yes,' said Gussie with unmistakable bitterness. 'And if you have your way, this quiet lane will be like a motorway and everyone will be driving along here like maniacs!'

'I was *not* driving like a maniac,' Hunter said grittily. 'It's true that I was anxious to get back to Bracklewick in time to go out to dinner, but I was hardly treating it as a motorway!' He stopped and peered more closely at Future Green's logo which was emblazoned across her wet chest. 'I should have guessed! You're one of the save-the-earth brigade with all the absurd ideas about Whin Farm, aren't you?'

Insensibly annoyed that he hadn't recognised her—she had recognised *him* at once!—Gussie shook her arm free of his grip and lifted her chin. 'If you mean, am I a member of the group dedicated to saving Whin Farm,

yes, I am!' she said grandly, and then spoilt the effect
by sitting down abruptly on the wet verge. 'I feel sick.'

Hunter was unsympathetic. 'It's just reaction,' he told
her in a brusque voice. He looked down at the slender,
bedraggled girl sitting among the long grass and the wild
flowers in the rain, her long legs splayed coltishly in front
of her. 'I remember you now. You were the spokesman—
whoops! *Spokesperson*—for the group.' He eyed her up
and down consideringly. 'You look much prettier with
your hair down.'

To her horror, Gussie blushed. She could feel his gaze
resting on the damp T-shirt which clung revealingly to
the soft curves of her figure, and she folded her arms
defensively across her chest.

'I'm not concerned about how I look,' she said stiffly.
'My only concern is the environment—and particularly
the future of Whin Farm.' Her unusual gold-flecked eyes
were huge in her white face as she looked up at him in
defiance, and the raindrops clung to her dark lashes.

'I'm sure it's all very worthy,' Hunter said, fore-
stalling her before she could launch into a passionate
defence of Whin Farm. 'But I've already listened to your
so-called concerns once this evening, and once is quite
enough. Besides,' he added dismissively, 'it's too wet to
stand here bandying views about the environment. You
may be happy getting back to nature, but my only
concern at the moment is getting warm and dry.' A
rumble of thunder overhead underlined his point.
'What's wrong with your bike?'

'The chain's come off,' Gussie said a little sullenly,
resenting the way he found it so easy to dismiss her arguments. 'I've just got to get it over the last cogs,' she

went on, in an effort to show him that she knew what she was doing.

Hunter glanced at her blackened hands. 'You seem to be having some difficulty. You'd better let me have a look.'

'It's all right, I can manage,' she snapped. 'You'd better go on if you're in such a big hurry to get back to Bracklewick!'

Ignoring her comment, Hunter bent down to inspect the chain which dangled uselessly from the cogs. 'You obviously haven't been managing very well so far,' he said astringently.

Gussie struggled to her feet and pushed the wet hair away from her face. 'I'd be OK if I just had something to use as a lever to get the last bit on. I've done it lots of times before.'

'If this has happened before, I would have thought it would have been a good idea to carry a tool with you,' Hunter pointed out with an irritable sigh. It was clear that he had far better things to do than stand around in the rain worrying about her bicycle. Straightening, he went round to the boot of his car. 'I expect I can find you something in my tool set.'

Of course, he *would* have a complete set of tools with him. Gussie felt unreasonably cross. 'Please don't bother,' she said stiffly, but Hunter took absolutely no notice of her. He came back holding a serviceable-looking screwdriver. 'This should do the trick. Would you like me to have a go?'

'I can do it!' Gussie practically snatched the screwdriver out of his hand.

The rain dripped down her neck as she crouched by the bike and fumbled with the chain. She could feel his critical eyes on her and she bit her lip. She had done this many times before; why wouldn't the wretched thing go on? Getting more and more cross and flustered, she jammed the screwdriver into place once more and yanked aggressively at the chain, which promptly snapped.

Gussie looked down at the broken chain lying on the wet tarmac. 'Oh,' she said.

Hunter gave an exasperated snort. 'That wasn't very helpful, was it?' he said acidly. 'Now what are you going to do?'

Cheeks burning with humiliation and the effort of wrestling with the chain, Gussie got to her feet and pushed the wet hair out of her eyes with her arm. She looked up and down the road as if in search of inspiration, but there was only the narrow country lane stretching emptily into the rain.

'I'll have to walk,' she said at last.

'In this?' Hunter glanced expressively at the pouring rain. He had turned the collar of his jacket up, but his wet hair was plastered to his head. 'You'll get soaked.'

'I'm soaked already,' Gussie pointed out, wiping the rain from her face with the flat of her hand, but her heart sank at the prospect of trudging all that way in the rain.

Hunter sighed. 'I'd better give you a lift. Where are you going?'

'Chitterburn,' said Gussie. 'But I don't need a lift, thank you. It's not far, I can easily walk.'

'Don't be ridiculous,' Hunter said irritably. 'I drove through Chitterburn on my way out from Bracklewick, and it must be at least five miles from here. I've got to go back that way anyway, so you may as well have a lift.' He opened the car door for her. 'Now come on, get in, before we both get any wetter.'

Gussie hesitated, eying the big black car dubiously. It looked comfortable and very fast, and probably gobbled up petrol, using up a non-renewable resource *and* polluting the atmosphere. It was exactly the kind of car she most disapproved of. On the other hand, it would get her home in a matter of minutes, and she was tired and cold and her feet were sore...

Hunter watched Gussie's expressive face. She had always had a secret yearning to be mysteriously enigmatic, but it was hopeless when you had a face that other people seemed to find as transparent as glass, and Hunter certainly had no trouble interpreting the struggle between her principles and her longing to be warm and dry. He rolled his eyes.

'I use unleaded petrol, if that makes you feel any better,' he said with exasperation.

'I'd rather walk,' Gussie said, lifting her chin proudly. She didn't want to be indebted to Hunter Scott!

'Don't tell me! Walking doesn't pollute the atmosphere?'

'Well, it doesn't,' she said defensively.

Hunter gave the impression of a man hanging on the shreds of his patience. 'Given that I'm going in the car anyway, the hole in the ozone layer isn't going to get any bigger if you come with me instead of plodding through the rain,' he pointed out with a distinct edge to his voice.

Gussie shifted uncomfortably. She was sorely tempted. 'You really don't need to bother...'

'The only bother is you dithering around in the rain while we both get wet,' he said trenchantly. 'Now, will you please stop being stupid and *get in*?'

There was an unmistakable note of authority in his voice, and Gussie found herself getting into the car without another word while Hunter put her bike in the boot. It even smelt expensive, she thought guiltily, pulling the heavy door to behind her and settling back into the luxurious seat. She felt decadent just sitting in a car like this, and dreaded to think what Simon would say if he could see her.

Hunter glanced at her as he got in beside her, and the car which had seemed so enormous appeared to shrink with his overwhelmingly solid presence. Suddenly Gussie was horribly conscious of her smudged face and filthy hands.

He had noticed them too. 'You're covered in oil,' he said. 'Here, use this to wipe your hands rather than my upholstery!'

Cross at being treated like a child, Gussie took the handkerchief he gave her and sulkily began to wipe the worst of the grease off her fingers. She wished he didn't have the ability to make her feel small and rather stupid.

'You and your group seem to know all about me, but who are you?' asked Hunter as he started the car. 'That aggressive young man called you Gus, but that can't be right, surely?'

'My name's Augusta,' Gussie said, trying to sound dignified.

'Augusta?' He raised one eyebrow. 'That's unusual.'

'I'm usually called Gussie,' she admitted. 'Augusta always sound so grand, and I'm not really a very grand sort of person.'

Hunter slanted a glance at her grubby face and the dark coppery hair hanging in dripping rat's-tails. Her eyes were lowered as she wrestled with the seatbelt, and the dark lashes swept down on to her cheeks.

'Somehow I didn't think you were,' he said.

Gussie had finally managed to click the seatbelt into place, and glanced up at the odd note in his voice, but he was looking straight ahead at the road before them. The windscreen-wipers swished hypnotically, and the car was so smooth that the tarmac seemed to flow effortlessly beneath them.

'How did you know I was coming this evening?' he asked after a pause.

His hair was dark and damp from the rain, and she could see raindrops on the shoulders of his tweed jacket. There was a faint roughness to his jaw as if he needed to shave, and Gussie found her eyes lingering on the point just below his ear. It gave her a strange feeling inside, and she looked away quickly.

'Bracklewick's a small place,' she answered evasively. Did he really think she was going to tell him who their informants were? She wasn't that much of a fool! 'It's easy to find out what's going on.'

'It's easy to get hold of the wrong end of the stick, too,' Hunter said with an ironic look. 'I'd advise you to do a little more research before you make any more wild accusations about my plans for Whin Farm.'

'We've done our research!' said Gussie, stung. 'You just don't want anyone to get in your way.'

'You seem to have a very melodramatic idea about how companies operate, Gussie,' he said acidly. 'Anyone would think our sole aim in life was to wreck the environment! Nothing could be further from the truth, I assure you.' He glanced at her as he changed down to round a sharp bend. 'Most companies are sensitive to public opinion, and Scott Developments is no exception, but public opinion isn't quite the same thing as a few muddle-headed protesters whipping up opposition with accusations that don't bear the slightest relation to the facts!'

'But we *know* the facts,' Gussie said stubbornly. 'The facts are that every day we're using up the resources of our planet, and unless we make a real effort to stop projects like yours it's going to be too late!'

'I agree that there are places where development has gone too far, but not even you could argue that Northumberland is one of them. It must be one of the most unspoilt parts of the country. If you feel that strongly about the environment, you'd be better off directing your efforts towards other areas where there's a much greater problem.'

'In other words, why don't we stop pestering you and go and make life difficult for someone else?'

Hunter's mouth twitched in reluctant appreciation. 'I wouldn't have put it quite like that, but yes, that's about it. You could do a lot more good than just getting in my way.'

Gussie stared out through the rain at the passing fields. He was right, in a way. There *were* other, more urgent causes, and there were times when she felt almost guilty at living in such a beautiful part of the country. 'We have to make sure Northumberland stays unspoilt,' she said at last. 'That's why I joined Future Green. They're fighting to save this area.' She turned slightly in her seat to face him, her eyes shining with conviction and her face vivid with passionate belief. 'Local issues matter just as much as national ones,' she told him. 'It's up to the bigger pressure groups to work on major problems. Our role—Future Green's role—is to try and change things on a local level. Perhaps it's not so dramatic, but every person you persuade to use a bottle bank, or switch off that extra light, makes a difference.'

She twisted the dirty handkerchief between her hands, desperate to try and make him understand. 'It's the same with Whin Farm. I know there are much more important problems in the world, but if you plough up the meadow there that's one more place where wild flowers won't grow any more. We have to say stop at some point. If we keep saying, Oh, it's not that important, it's only one or two fields and no one will bother, before we know where we are we won't have any wild flowers left at all! And it's not just flowers. If we don't make a real effort to save them, we won't have any old woods or any butterflies or any wild animals.'

Gussie paused for breath, and Hunter threw her a sideways look.

'You know, you're much more persuasive now than when you were brandishing threats and placards! I thought you looked unconvinced about what you were doing. What's a girl like you doing with such a militant group?'

He was straight-faced, but Gussie sensed that he was somehow amused. She couldn't quite pin down how she knew. There was no smile, no tell-tale smirk. Perhaps it was the suggestion of a crinkle at the edges of his eyes, or an imperceptible deepening of the crease at the corner of his mouth? It was impossible to tell, but she was sure that he was secretly laughing at her.

'I'm militant too!' she protested, affronted. She was tired of not being taken seriously, of being told that she didn't belong in the group! It was true that she had always hated rows, and one of the things she loved about animals was that they were so much less aggressive than humans, but it didn't mean that she wasn't prepared to stand up and fight for what she believed in.

Hunter shook his head. 'No, you're not. I don't mean you don't care about the environment. You obviously do, probably more than any of them, but you don't seem to be a naturally aggressive person. I should have said you were...' He paused, searching for the right word, and then glanced at her again, his expression thoughtful. 'I should have said you were passionate rather than militant.'

Gussie felt the breath tighten in her throat, and she stared at the windscreen-wipers, gripped by a sudden paralysing shyness. She was very aware of his hands on the steering-wheel, and the controlled strength of his body. There was an undeniable magnetism about him, but the more she fought against it, the more hot and flustered she felt.

'I'm tougher than I look,' she muttered, but the next moment she gasped and clapped her hands to her eyes as a tiny, elegant stoat bounded into the road in front of the car. 'Watch out!'

Hunter sighed. 'It's all right, you can look.'

'You didn't hit it, did you?' Gussie lowered her hands cautiously.

'Of course I didn't hit it!' he said, with a return to his irritable manner. 'I thought you said you were tough!'

'Not about animals,' she admitted. 'Cars are such murderous things. The roads are littered with little bodies. Rabbits and hedgehogs and birds, all mown down by people driving too fast to care.' She looked accusingly at the speedometer. 'Once I saw a crow who'd just been run over, and its mate kept trying to help it up. It was as if he wouldn't accept that she was dead.' Gussie shuddered at the memory. 'It was awful.'

'You can't afford to be too sentimental, Gussie,' Hunter said in a dry voice. 'Things aren't black and white. Yes, cars pollute the atmosphere. Yes, they sometimes knock down rabbits, not to mention people, but they're convenient. We all like living in a home where you can switch on an electric light if it's dark, or use a washing-machine instead of scrubbing everything by hand. These things improve the quality of our lives. Nobody wants to give them up.'

'I know that,' said Gussie, wishing that Simon were there. He knew how to argue cleverly with people like Hunter. She was always left with a muddled sense of what was and wasn't right, and a total inability to explain exactly what she felt. She turned the handkerchief between her hands. 'I just think people should be more aware of their environment and how they can affect it.'

It was with some relief that she spotted the church tower through the trees as the big car swept effortlessly round the narrow bends towards Chitterburn. Hunter Scott made her feel edgy and uncertain.

The next moment they were running quietly into the village. Chitterburn was an attractive place, with unpretentious square houses built in the local ivory-grey stone and set off by the bright colours of the traditional cottage flowers which were reviving visibly in the rain after a long dry spell. There was hardly anyone about. Rain and tea had kept them all indoors, and Gussie was grateful that there would be no one to witness her arrival in just the kind of car she was usually protesting about!

'If you drop me at the post office, that'll be fine,' she said stiffly. 'I just live round the corner.' For someone who had decided that Hunter was a typically sneering, bullying developer, she was curiously reluctant to get out of his car. As she opened the door, she told herself it was because she had been unable to convince him to change his mind about Whin Farm.

Hunter had already lifted the bike out of the boot and had set it on its wheels. Gussie took hold of the handlebars and her nerves tightened alarmingly as his hands brushed against hers.

'Thank you,' she muttered. She longed suddenly to say something clever, to make him look at her properly, to see her as a girl instead of a dirty and mildly irritating protester. Simon would have been able to think of some clever comment so that he could walk away with the last word, but all she could do was to look uncertainly down at the handkerchief, covered in oil and balled tightly in her hand. 'Er—here's your handkerchief.' Hardly a great exit line, she realised, dispirited, as she held it out to him.

Hunter shoved it into his pocket. 'Dare I say goodbye, or are you planning to protest on my doorstep until Whin Farm is developed?' His voice held the now familiar exasperated edge, but when she looked into the slate-blue eyes Gussie saw a glint of unmistakable amusement and her chin came up in instinctive reaction.

'You'll certainly be seeing me again,' she said, taking refuge in what she hoped was a haughty indifference. 'The only way you'll get rid of me is by leaving Whin Farm alone!'

Hunter looked down into her face, and the mockery in his eyes was very pronounced. 'Well, now, is that a threat or a promise, I wonder?'

'A threat!' snapped Gussie, abandoning her attempts to sound lofty.

'I think it's high time someone taught you a lesson,' he said softly, taking her chin in one strong hand. Taken by surprise, Gussie nearly dropped the bike and clutched at it to stop it falling, leaving her without a hand to push him away. She stared mutely up at him, her golden eyes defiant and a little frightened. His gaze might hold amusement, but there was a ruthless set to his mouth, and she knew that it was useless to struggle.

'You need to learn that I don't take kindly to being threatened,' he went on, in the same implacable tone. His eyes were speculative as they looked down into hers. 'There are much better things to care passionately about than the environment, Augusta. Have you learnt that yet, or do I need to teach you that too?'

At that, Gussie did try to pull away, but it was too late. Hunter's fingers tightened against her face, and then he bent his head and captured her mouth with his own.

Gussie had the strangest feeling that the world had stopped and arrowed into one point of piercing awareness, and she forgot to struggle. Her lips parted involuntarily beneath the warm persuasion of his mouth, and he brought his other hand up to slide beneath her hair and caress the stubborn line of her jaw with his thumb.

Unthinkingly, still clutching at the handlebars, she leant towards him across the bike so that the kiss could deepen. The touch of his mouth had lit an unsuspected flame deep within her which leapt and scorched at her senses, taking them to a pitch of feeling Gussie had only dreamt of before, and she was shaken and disorientated when Hunter lifted his head. She didn't know if the kiss had lasted for seconds, or minutes, or hours. All she knew was that her body still burned with the memory of his touch.

'I hope you've learnt the first lesson as well as you've obviously learnt the second,' Hunter said, and there was a humiliating undercurrent of laughter in his voice.

Gussie stared up at him as the realisation of what she had done slowly sank in. This was Hunter Scott, the man she had sworn to oppose, the worst kind of developer, who represented everything she despised, and she had let him kiss her, without even a struggle. Worse, she had *enjoyed* it.

And instead of apologising all *he* could do was stand there with those hatefully mocking eyes, as if he knew perfectly well what she was thinking and thought it was funny!

Gussie struggled to pull herself together. She longed to lash out with some stinging retort, but in the end all she could come up with was an, 'Oh . . . oh,' of mingled frustration and mortification before she gave in and fled with her bike.

Once out of sight, she stopped and tried to calm down. Her cheeks burned, remembering how she had leant against him. She could still feel the pressure of his lips and the deep, quivering excitement of his kiss, and her scalp tingled at the memory.

Behind the post office, she could hear the car start and drive off unhurriedly and imagined Hunter grinning to himself at her naïve reaction to his kiss. Gussie's hands clenched around the handlebars. If he thought his 'lessons' had been a success, she would soon change his mind! She wouldn't give him the satisfaction of knowing how much it had affected her, she decided, pride coming to her rescue. She took a few deep breaths. It was only a kiss. He had no business to take her by surprise like that. If—when—they next met, she would treat him with the contempt he deserved and ignore the whole incident.

It wasn't so easy to ignore the way her body still tingled from his touch, and she was afraid that the lingering thrill of her senses would somehow show in her face, but fortunately her mother was standing at the door, in mid-conversation with her father in another room, and didn't notice Gussie as she eased off her sodden trainers at the kitchen door.

Now that she was so close to being dry, she realised how wet she was. She had been so taken up with Hunter Scott that she hadn't realised quite how uncomfortably her jeans clung or how the hair dripped down her neck. She grimaced as she squelched into the kitchen in her wet socks.

'What time is he coming?' her mother was calling through the door, but the reply was muffled. 'Half-past what?'

'Seven,' said Gussie, who had better hearing than her mother. 'What time is who coming?' she asked, shutting the door behind her.

'An old colleague of your father's.' Margaret Blake wiped her hands on a tea-towel. 'Apparently they used to work together in the Middle East and they bumped into each other in Bracklewick of all places this morning. He's——' She broke off as she took in Gussie's dripping appearance. 'Augusta! What on earth have you been doing?'

'The chain's broken on my bike again.' Gussie avoided her eyes, and made a fuss of the two dogs who had bustled up to her to say hello. Her mother was a little too sharp at noticing things. 'I had to push it home.'

'You'd better go and have a bath before this man arrives,' said her mother, clicking her tongue in concern. 'And do you think you could put a dress on instead of those old jeans of yours?'

'Oh, all right.' Gussie sighed. Her mother was always trying to make her look more feminine. She plodded up to the landing and then stopped short as she caught sight of herself in the long mirror. A wide-eyed girl with bedraggled hair and smears of black oil all over her face stared back at her, appalled. She looked an absolute mess. No wonder Hunter Scott had been unimpressed! Gussie remembered the mocking glint in his eyes and bit her lip as she realised what he must have thought of her—a grubby schoolgirl lecturing him on the environment. Next time she met him, she vowed, she would show him just how wrong he had been!

CHAPTER THREE

IT WAS bliss to step into a hot bath. She had been trying to persuade her parents that a shower would use much less water, but for once she was glad that they had refused to get rid of the traditional bath.

Submerged in the hot water, Gussie contemplated her toes and wondered what Hunter Scott was doing. He would be back at Bracklewick by now. What was he doing this evening that had him in such a hurry to get back? Who would he be with?

Her mind drifted, lulled by the fragrant steam from the bath. She could visualise him so clearly that he might have been standing in front of her. That forceful profile, the decisive line of his jaw, the way he had turned his head to look at her in the car, his hand resting on the gear lever as he changed down to round a bend, that devastating mouth... Gussie's eyes focused suddenly on her curling toes and she jerked them beneath the water with a splash.

Reaching for a towel, she got out of the bath abruptly and rubbed herself dry with unnecessary vigour. She was *not* going to think about that kiss. Her eye fell on a poster she had pinned up years ago, urging action to save the seas, and she squared her shoulders. She had more important concerns.

To keep her mother happy, she pulled on a cotton dress and dragged a comb through her tangled hair. Normally, she wouldn't have given another thought to her appearance, but tonight for some reason she paused in front of the mirror. The thick copper-coloured hair was already beginning to dry in a cloud about her heart-shaped face. Would Hunter Scott think she looked quite so ridiculous now?

Gussie leant forward to inspect her reflection critically. Why had she never realised quite how unflattering this dress was before? It was a dull purply grey colour, shapeless apart from a drawstring at the waist, but there was no point in changing, even if she had had anything better to wear. After all, it was only some old engineering colleague of her father's coming to dinner. He wouldn't care what she wore.

Mentally blocking out the dress, Gussie studied her face. Scrubbed of oil and grease, the fine skin held a translucent glow. She would never look sophisticated with that wide mouth and those freckles over her nose, but the high cheekbones and dark slanting brows suggested at a hint of the exotic that sat oddly with the guileless look in her clear eyes. The colour of good whisky, they gazed limpidly back at Gussie from the mirror, until she realised what she was doing. She had never worried about what she looked like before. Why should one meeting with Hunter Scott have her peering anxiously into the mirror and wondering if her dress suited her or not?

Determined to put him out of her mind, Gussie went out on to the landing. Half-past seven, she noted, glancing at the old grandfather clock over the banisters, but there was no sign of her father's friend. If she were lucky, she would have time to ring Simon before Mark got in with his version of events.

Gussie slipped along to her parents' bedroom. The phone there was much more private than the one in the hall, where her brothers could overhear what she was saying and tease her unmercifully afterwards.

'How did you get on with Scott?' Simon asked when he answered the phone.

'Well . . .' Gussie hesitated. It wouldn't do to tell him quite how disastrously the confrontation had gone. 'I told him we weren't going to stand by and let him ruin Whin Farm.' That was true enough.

'Good, good. And how did he react?'

'He didn't seem very impressed,' Gussie had to admit. Remembering the mocking look in Hunter's grey-blue eyes, 'not impressed' was something of an understatement. 'He said he was going to make every effort to preserve the environment.'

Simon sighed. 'You didn't believe him, I hope, Gus! You know what these companies are like. They'll say anything if they think it'll be good PR, but when it comes to making a profit they soon forget all their fine words.'

'I know,' said Gussie humbly. 'But I think we're going to have to be careful about how we approach Hunter Scott. I just get the feeling that he won't be an easy man to cross.' She could still feel the effect of those hard eyes boring into her.

'In that case, perhaps I'd better take over this project.'

Gussie could have kicked herself. Simon talked a lot about the democratic process, but he always seemed to find an excuse to take charge sooner or later. She had been stupid to give him such an obvious reason to shunt

her back to collecting signatures for a petition or sticking
up posters.

'I can do it,' she said quickly.

'Are you sure, Gus? Remember, I've got a bit more
experience than you. I know how to handle men like
Scott. We were used to dealing with hot-shot busi-
nessmen when I worked in London.'

Had that condescending note been in Simon's voice
before, or had she only just noticed it? With a small
shock of surprise, Gussie realised that for once she wasn't
that impressed by being reminded of Simon's job with
one of the big environmental pressure groups.

'You said I could lead this project,' she said. 'I know
I can do it.' She searched around wildly for some way
to convince him she had thought the whole thing
through. 'I'm going to try and see him alone to see if I
can persuade him of our arguments before we try any
more demonstrations.'

'I don't think that'll do much good. He's not likely
to listen to you, is he?'

'He might,' said Gussie firmly. She was quite sure that
Hunter would be unmoved by demonstrations, but she
didn't expect Simon to believe her. 'I want to try anyway.
If I'm leading this project, I want to do it my way.'

She had always been too intimidated by the trendiness
of Future Green's central clique to be so outspoken
before, and she could feel Simon's surprise at her sudden
assertiveness. Gussie was surprised herself. Why *was* she
so determined? she wondered, and decided that it was
a perfectly natural desire to show Hunter Scott that
she wasn't a silly little girl who could be scared off by
a mere kiss.

'Oh, very well,' Simon was saying, with an indulgent laugh. 'We'll let you have one more go, but after that I think Mark or I should take over the protest. Whin Farm is too important to fall into developers' hands.'

'It won't,' Gussie promised.

'OK, then. Right.' It was Simon's favourite phrase. He used it all the time in meetings, and it had become something of a catchword at Future Green. Gussie had never been able to say it with quite the right kind of trendily laid-back intonation. Simon's voice changed slightly. 'Are you coming in tomorrow?' he asked, a shade too casually. 'We still need people to collect signatures for the petition against the new road at Ribersham.'

Gussie suppressed a sigh. She had done more than her share of collecting signatures for the last petition. 'We're terribly busy at the restaurant at the moment,' she said. 'I promised Tony I'd do an evening and a lunchtime shift tomorrow...' She trailed off, and then relented, feeling guilty at her lack of commitment. 'I could come in for a couple of hours in the afternoon if you like.'

'Can't you get the evening off?' Simon lowered his voice. 'I thought maybe we could go out and have a meal, just the two of us, you know.'

Gussie looked down at the receiver in her hand in some surprise. She had admired Simon from afar ever since she had joined Future Green. He was so intense, so dedicated, so committed that he had given up a good job in London to come back and work at grass-roots level. She had been longing for him to show an interest in her, but now that he had she felt strangely less than thrilled.

'I'd have liked that,' she said carefully, 'but I can't tomorrow, I'm afraid. Tony's short-staffed as it is, and he's already given me this evening off so that I could go up to Whin Farm.'

'I don't know why you're so loyal to Tony Marcello.' There was a peevish edge to Simon's voice. 'You shouldn't be working for someone who admits so freely that his only interest is making money.'

'He's just joking,' Gussie defended her boss. 'He doesn't mean it. He's terribly nice when you get to know him, really. He's even started offering a vegetarian dish of the day!'

'Well, I wouldn't work for him,' said Simon grandly. 'My conscience wouldn't let me.'

'I have to earn some money somehow,' she protested. 'I can't just live off my parents while I'm working voluntarily for Future Green.'

'The trouble with you, Gus, is that you're too much part of the system . . .' Gussie listened with half an ear while Simon held forth about his theories. Downstairs, the doorbell rang and she could hear her father greeting his friend.

What was wrong with her? Normally she would have hung on Simon's every word, but somehow whenever she tried to picture his thin, intense face she would see Hunter Scott's strong features instead.

'I'm sorry, Simon, I'll really have to go,' she interrupted him in the end, and put down the phone thankfully when he had said a reluctant goodbye. He hated to be interrupted when he was explaining one of his theories.

Gussie pulled her fingers through her hair, wishing suddenly that she'd never set eyes on Hunter Scott. She had been perfectly happy before, but one brief meeting had thrown her oddly off balance, leaving her uncertain and confused.

She glanced at herself in the mirror, as if to check that she was the same girl who had cycled so confidently up to Whin Farm that evening. The cloud of soft hair was the same, so were the wide, clear eyes and the slender figure. There was no reason to think that she was any different now.

But she was. She had been kissed by Hunter Scott.

It wasn't as if it was her first kiss, she thought, obscurely resentful, but no other kiss had electrified her senses that way, leaving them tingling and alert and turning her upside-down. The trouble was, she didn't *want* to be different. She wanted to be the way she had been before she met Hunter Scott. She had been so certain about what she thought and what she felt. It wasn't fair that he should unsettle her with one stupid kiss. Gussie's golden eyes lit with sudden rebellion. She wouldn't let herself be changed. She would put Hunter out of her mind, and carry on just as she had before!

Determined to do just that, Gussie ran lightly downstairs to greet her father's guest. Still thinking of Hunter, she was unconscious of the tilt to her chin or the defiant sparkle in her eyes as she opened the sitting-room door and stopped dead on the threshold in stunned surprise.

He was standing by the fireplace, holding a glass and talking to her mother. He stopped as the door opened and one dark brow shot up in surprise as he looked over to where Gussie stood frozen with disbelief. It *couldn't* be!

But there was the same distinctive presence, the same relaxed stance that somehow did nothing to decrease the impression of toughness, the same slate-coloured eyes. The same mouth. It *was* Hunter Scott.

'Ah, here's my daughter,' said her father. 'Augusta, this is Hunter Scott.'

Gussie had a tight, breathless feeling, as if she had been punched in the stomach, and her heart was lurching alarmingly. How could Hunter Scott be here?

'Augusta?' John Blake prompted her, puzzled by Gussie's silence.

'Hello.' Gussie was horrified at how thin and high her voice sounded. Desperately trying to pull herself together, she forced herself to walk across to where Hunter stood. Why didn't he say something? Had he even recognised her? The thought that he might have put her completely out of his mind gave her a welcome burst of anger, and her eyes were hostile as she looked up at him at last.

He had recognised her all right. He had recovered quickly from his surprise at seeing her, and the blue-grey eyes glinted. Gussie would have liked to think that he was discomfited to find that the girl he had kissed so humiliatingly was none other than the daughter of his old friend, but she strongly suspected that he was merely amused.

There was an odd little pause while they looked at each other, and then Hunter smiled and held out his hand.

'Hello.'

Aware of her parents' curious looks, Gussie had no choice but to shake his hand. His strong fingers closed around hers and she felt a bolt of lightning reaction jolt up her arm. His hand was warm and firm, and the touch of their palms seemed unbearably intimate. Gussie drew her hand away with a tiny intake of breath and moved blindly to a chair.

Her hand felt as if it was burning with the memory of his touch. Gussie wanted to hold it carefully, but for the first time she realised that her two younger brothers, Drew and Gavin, were in the room, and that they were watching her with quick, speculative eyes. Anxious not to draw attention to herself, Gussie forced herself to leave her hand casually on the arm of the chair, where it felt hot and awkward and conspicuous.

Dimly, she could hear her father explaining how he and Hunter had met on a project in the Middle East. She hoped that if she sat still enough no one would notice how oddly she was behaving. Her heart was still slamming against her ribs, but more slowly now, and she risked a glance at Hunter.

He was sipping his drink as he listened courteously to her father, turning to include Drew and Gavin in the conversation. Gussie was struck afresh at his self-possession. While she looked tense and self-conscious, Hunter was relaxed, charming. It wasn't fair. *He* was the one who ought to be embarrassed!

He was taking no notice of her whatsoever, Gussie realised with perverse resentment. Was 'hello' all he was going to say? Why didn't he admit that they'd already met? Why didn't he look at her, instead of chatting easily with Drew and Gavin as if he was really interested in what they had to say?

At that moment, Hunter glanced over to find her watching him. Gussie found herself staring into his eyes, unable to look away. The memory of his mouth was painfully vivid. She could taste his lips and feel the tantalising brush of his fingers. Looking into his eyes now, she saw the amusement deepen, and knew that he knew perfectly well what she was thinking about. The hot, treacherous colour washed up her cheeks as she turned her head deliberately away.

'I always said you were far too capable to stay with that firm,' her father was saying. 'Not nearly enough scope for a man of your talents. What are you doing now?'

'I've got my own company developing projects, mostly in the UK but I'm hoping to expand our international operation. There's a chance of a big project in Brazil coming up which should give us a good foothold in South America.' Hunter took a sip of his drink. 'The head office is in London, but I tend to do a lot of travelling, sorting out the inevitable problems at the start of a project and setting things up locally before the building begins.'

'Bracklewick seems an unlikely place for a man of your experience,' Margaret Blake commented. 'What are you doing up here?'

Gussie sat silently, staring at the carriage clock on the mantelpiece and willing the colour to fade from her face. She couldn't look at him, but she felt Hunter glance towards her.

'I've got an interest in a place called Whin Farm as a possible site for a new leisure complex,' he said carefully.

'Oh, Jack Wilson will be pleased!' cried her mother. 'He's been desperate to sell the farm for a long time now. Is this a definite plan?'

Gussie's face was set. Her parents knew that she was involved with Future Green, but she suspected that they didn't really approve, and she never discussed their protests at home. They would be horrified to think that she had threatened to obstruct Hunter's plans.

'The agreement's not finalised yet,' Hunter said. 'But we're certainly hoping the deal will go through if there are no last-minute problems.'

'I hope so too,' said her mother. 'Jack's longing to be able to retire and go and live with his daughter. He hasn't felt the same about Whin Farm since his wife died. You're not anticipating any problems, are you?'

Hunter glanced at Gussie again. 'Not any real problems, no. There are usually a few minor irritations to sort out, that's all.'

Gussie knew perfectly well that his comment was directed at her. So that was how he thought of her, a 'minor irritation'? She glared at him, and he met her eyes with a mocking look.

'It's hard to imagine Whin Farm as a leisure complex,' Drew said.

'Country club might be a better description,' said Hunter, mockery vanishing as he turned away from Gussie. 'More and more people are interested in the countryside, but it can be quite difficult to get at. Farmers don't want people trampling over their fields and there often isn't anywhere to stop, so we've been building a chain of complexes in rural areas. The idea is to provide sporting facilities like swimming-pool, tennis courts and golf course and so on, as well as the chance to fish or shoot. We put in extensive trails for those who like to walk, and there's a restaurant, bar and adventure playground so that whole families can spend a day in the country doing whatever they like. They can buy a day's membership which allows access to all the facilities, but we've found that lots of people prefer to just walk in the woods, or sit in a meadow without being chased off by a farmer. The more established clubs have proved so popular that we've put in accommodation as well, and people spend whole holidays without ever leaving the grounds.'

'It sounds great,' Gavin enthused. 'I wouldn't mind being able to go and spend a day somewhere like that.'

'Me neither,' said Drew. 'Everyone always thinks it must be wonderful to live in the country, but the fact is that there's never anything to do.'

'It's enough just to be in the country!' Gussie said, unable to keep quiet any longer. 'You and Gavin don't know how lucky you are to be able to walk out and see the wild flowers along the hedgerows, or smell the hay, or breathe in the clean air! All you want are *facilities*! Personally, I can't think of anything worse than spending a day crammed in with a lot of other people in what some property developers from London think is the countryside! I think it sounds ghastly,' she added with a defiant look at Hunter. 'I suppose you're going to put some plastic cows in the fields too, to add to the natural effect?'

'Augusta!' Her parents frowned, and the boys rolled their eyes.

Far from being offended, Hunter looked amused at her outburst. 'The clubs aren't to everyone's taste,' he said. 'But many people enjoy them very much. As for plastic cows, I can assure you there's no likelihood of my agreeing to anything of the kind.' He paused. 'You'd probably approve if you ever visited one of our clubs.'

'I doubt it!' Gussie was still looking mutinous. His restrained reply had made her sound strident, she knew, but she couldn't help it. Hunter's presence made her edgy and she was horribly conscious of the fact that her dress didn't suit her at all.

'Shall we go and eat?' Margaret Blake interposed calmly, and the subject was forgotten as they moved into the dining-room. 'Yours is in the oven, dear,' she added in an undertone to Gussie as she began to serve the casserole. She had always been very understanding about Gussie's vegetarianism, and made her a separate meal whenever they were going to have meat.

'Here comes Gussie with her nut cutlet!' Drew chortled as she reappeared with her vegetable lasagne. It didn't matter what she had, he and Gavin always said the same thing. Normally, Gussie ignored them, but today, with Hunter sitting opposite her, her cheeks flamed.

'You're not alone,' he said. 'More and more people are giving up meat. We make sure that there's a wide variety of vegetarian meals available at the clubs.'

'Big of you!' Gussie snapped, too unnerved to recognise his attempt to divert attention away from her.

Gavin leant towards Hunter confidingly. 'Gussie's our local eccentric, as you've probably gathered. Everyone in Chitterburn thinks she's loopy.'

'No, they don't!' Margaret Blake protested, glancing from her daughter's tense face to the man opposite her. His expression gave nothing away.

Drew chimed in in support of his brother. 'Yes, they do, Mother! Remember that time when Gussie went round every single house in the village and insisted on collecting that day's junk mail so she could send it back with a protest note saying how many trees had been cut down to provide the paper?'

'Or when she tackled old Phil Beadle in the pub about the way he treated his dog? What a scene that was!'

'And the next minute she was lecturing everyone on how we could save the output of one nuclear power station a year if only people wouldn't fill their kettles to the brim every time they boiled some water! *That* was embarrassing!'

'If it weren't for Augusta, we wouldn't have our own bottle bank in the village,' her mother said loyally.

Gussie stared down at her vegetable lasagne, mortified. She wished her brothers would shut up. Hunter would think she was too silly for words, if he didn't already! She was overwhelmingly conscious of his hands holding his knife and fork on the other side of the table, and his mouth kept tugging at the top of her vision.

'Once,' said Gavin, getting into his stride, 'she even refused to go on holiday. Do you remember that, Drew?' He turned to Hunter to explain. 'We were due to go off to Corfu, but Gussie insisted on staying to keep a twenty-four hour vigil over some flower which she said was the

rarest in the country. She dragged some poor woman
from the Botanical Society all the way up here, only to
find that it was just a cowslip!'

'It wasn't a cowslip!' Gussie said, as he and Drew
laughed heartily at the memory. Her parents were smiling
and Hunter's mouth quirked, as if he found the story
as entertaining as everyone else. 'It was a wild orchid,'
she explained defiantly, 'and they *are* rare. It's just that
it wasn't the lady's slipper orchid that I thought it was.
That's only found in one place in Britain now, so if it
had been one it would have been terribly important that
no one touch it.'

'You obviously take your concern for the environment very seriously,' Hunter said gravely, but the
laughter danced in his slate-blue eyes. Gussie decided
that she preferred him when he was hard and ruthless.
It was easier to remember what he was really like that
way.

'She takes it too seriously,' grumbled her father. 'She
spends her whole time with some green protest group
instead of using her brain in a proper job. You'd better
watch out, Hunter, or they'll be on to you and your
Whin Farm plans!'

There was a tiny pause. Involuntarily, Gussie glanced
at Hunter, wondering if he would tell her parents how
she had sworn to oppose him. He was watching her consideringly, but as she stared at him, a mute plea in her
gold-flecked eyes, he smiled.

'I'll be on my guard,' he said lightly.

The sudden, unshadowed warmth of his smile caught
at Gussie's breath. He hadn't smiled at her like that
before, and she had the strangest feeling that she was

floating above her chair. The smile transformed him; she barely recognised the hard, irritable man who had given her a lift home in the stranger who sat opposite her, and she was overwhelmed by a rush of awareness. She wanted desperately to reach over and touch him, and, confused by her own conflicting reactions to him, she flushed and jerked her eyes away.

'You don't need to worry about Augusta,' her father was saying comfortably. 'She's got too warm a heart to be a real fanatic, however much she pretends otherwise, but that Simon Mansfield is another matter.'

'Simon Mansfield?' Hunter lifted an eyebrow in polite enquiry.

'He's the chairperson of Future Green,' Gussie said stiffly. She didn't want to talk about Simon, especially not to Hunter.

'Gussie's got a crush on him,' Drew said helpfully. 'I can't think why. He's so *intense*.'

'Yeah, intensely boring!' added Gavin. 'Simon can tell you exactly how many species of insect have become extinct since the Ice Age, or how to make organic wine.'

'At least Simon cares about the environment and does something about it,' Gussie said hotly, provoked into defending him, even though the accusation that he was boring had struck an uncomfortably hollow note. Hunter's smile had vanished as if it had never been. It had just been a smile, she tried to tell herself, gulping at her wine. Just a stretching of a mouth, a crinkling round the eye. That was all.

There was an awkward silence, broken by her father in a jovial attempt to change the subject.

'How's your wife, Hunter?'

Gussie choked on her wine, and Gavin thumped her back as she coughed and spluttered. 'Went down the wrong way,' she tried to explain in a hoarse voice, and bent her head over her plate so that neither of her brothers would be tempted to ask embarrassing questions about why the mention of Hunter's wife should have such a dramatic effect. She felt as if someone had hit her. Hunter, *married*? Why had it never occurred to her? And why did she feel so desolate at the thought?

'I'm not married,' said Hunter calmly when Gussie's splutters had subsided.

Giddy relief sang along Gussie's veins, but she didn't dare look at him. He had an uncomfortable habit of seeming to know exactly what she was thinking.

'Oh? Er——' her father was looking embarrassed '—I rather thought that you and that very attractive girl who used to work for Brian Gates...'

'Imogen?' Even though she wasn't watching him, Gussie sensed his withdrawal. 'We were together for a few years, but we never married. I haven't seen her for some time. When I came back to London, we agreed to go our separate ways.'

It was clear that he didn't want to talk about Imogen. Gussie was ashamed of her own curiosity. She stared down into her glass and wondered just what lay behind Hunter's bleak account. Why hadn't they ever married? Why had they broken up? What was Imogen like? Did Hunter still love her?

Her father answered at least one of her questions. 'I'm sorry to hear that,' he said with gruff sympathy. 'She was a fine-looking girl. Always beautifully dressed, and very capable too, if I remember right.'

Hunter's eyes flickered briefly to Gussie. 'Yes, she was.'

Well, at least she knew that, whatever had prompted that kiss, it hadn't been irresistible attraction. Judging by her father's description of Imogen, she was the complete opposite of the kind of girl Hunter found attractive, Gussie thought dolefully. He had wanted to humiliate her, to show her just how little her opposition worried him, and he had succeeded.

Gussie ate her way silently through the interminable meal. Across the table, Hunter was being an ideal guest, and the rest of her family clearly enjoyed his company, but she felt somehow isolated from it all, miserably conscious of her frumpy dress and the fact that she would never be attractive or smart or capable, or any of the things that Hunter obviously admired in a woman. She remembered bitterly how determined she had been to show him that she wasn't as gauche and silly as he thought her. She didn't stand a chance, not against the memory of the unknown girl called Imogen. But what did it matter, after all? She didn't care what kind of girl Hunter liked. She didn't even *like* him.

The meal seemed to go on forever, but at last they went back through to the sitting-room for coffee. Only a few more minutes, Gussie told herself, and then it would be over. She wanted nothing more than to go to bed and have a good cry, though she wasn't at all sure what she would be crying about. She only knew that she felt miserable and unsettled and awkward and ugly.

'We must have some of these lovely chocolates you brought, Hunter,' Margaret Blake said, handing him a cup of coffee and turning back to pick up the chocolates. 'Look, Gussie, they're your favourites.'

Gussie eyed the box longingly. They were indeed her favourites. Her guilty weakness for expensive chocolates was a source of much amusement to her brothers.

'I don't think you should, Gussie!' Gavin tut-tutted as he saw her hesitate. 'You know Simon wouldn't approve! Look at all that unnecessary packaging! All those chocolates individually wrapped—what a waste of paper! And that plastic box! It's not at all biodegradable, is it?'

Gussie shifted uncomfortably. He was teasing, but he was right. Simon certainly wouldn't approve. And yet she was sure a chocolate would make her feel much better. Surely one couldn't do any harm? Her mouth watered at the prospect, even while her conscience nagged, reminding her of her principles.

They were all laughing as they watched her agony of indecision. Eventually, Hunter got up and took the box of chocolates from her mother. He took the lid off and offered the box to Gussie.

'I insist on you having one. Tell your conscience I forced you!'

His smile was irresistible. Gussie decided that she liked him after all. 'Well, if I must...!' She took one with a grateful look. 'Thank you.'

'Don't feel guilty about it,' he said. 'We've all got a weakness, after all.'

Unwrapping her chocolate, Gussie glanced up at him under her lashes. 'What's yours?' she asked daringly.

Hunter hesitated. He looked down into her topaz eyes and his smile twisted slightly. 'That would be telling,' he said.

CHAPTER FOUR

THE next night was busier than usual in Tony's wine bar, and Gussie rushed backwards and forwards between the tables with bottles of wine and baskets of garlic bread and elaborate hamburgers. She wore jeans and a plain white T-shirt beneath a short waiter's apron, and her hair fell in a tumble of copper to her shoulders.

'I'm exhausted already, and it's only nine o'clock,' she gasped, collapsing against the bar while she waited for Tony to get her order of drinks.

'You do too much, Gussie,' said Tony. 'I know how hard you work here, and you seem to spend the rest of your time doing the dirty work for those green friends of yours. You should give yourself a break sometimes, or you'll wear yourself out.'

'I can't take a break now,' Gussie said, appalled at the idea of such disloyalty.

'Why not? I know you're bent on saving the world single-handed, but it'll survive without you for a few days, surely?'

Gussie eyed him with some hostility. 'You sound like Hunter Scott!'

'Who's he?' asked Tony, opening another bottle of wine with an expert flourish. 'With a name like Hunter, he's presumably not a member of Future Green!'

'He most certainly isn't!' said Gussie tartly. 'He's about as green as you are!'

Tony grinned. 'Oh, dear. That bad?' He was very fond of Gussie and regarded her obsession with Future Green with tolerant amusement mixed with some exasperation.

'He's a developer,' she explained with loathing and Tony gave a mock-gasp, crossing his forefingers in a mocking gesture to ward off evil. Gussie ignored him. 'He's buying Whin Farm from Jack Wilson. He wants to turn it into a leisure complex of all things!'

'Let me guess!' Tony cried, holding up a hand. 'Future Green don't approve?'

'Of course we don't! Whin Farm is a very valuable site.'

'But I thought poor old Jack had let everything go?'

'That's precisely why it's so valuable—in ecological terms anyway. There are parts of Whin Farm that have hardly been touched by modern farming methods, and we're determined that it's not going be bulldozed by Hunter Scott.'

'So you're going to fight him?'

'Every inch of the way!' said Gussie, tilting her chin and trying to forget how inadequate she had felt when faced with the sheer force of Hunter's personality. 'That's why I can't take a holiday just now. I'm in charge of the protest,' she added proudly. 'Future Green are relying on me to make sure that Scott doesn't get away with his plans.'

Tony finished pouring the wine carefully into three of the glasses. 'I still think you're too nice a girl to be involved with that lot. If you ask me, they take advantage of you.' He squirted soda into the fourth glass and dropped in a slice of lemon and some ice. 'Here, get rid of this, and then be a love and take table two's order, will you? I gave them the menus, but I haven't had a chance to get back to them yet, and Jane's still waiting for that big party in the corner to make up their minds.'

Gussie nodded and picked up the tray of drinks. As soon as she had taken them over, she dropped the tray back on the bar and made her way over to other side of the restaurant. Jane, the other waitress, normally dealt with the tables on this side, but they often helped each other out when things were busy. Table two was tucked over in the far corner, half hidden by an enormous potted palm, and Gussie was too busy burrowing in the pocket of her apron for order book and pencil to notice who was sitting there until she was right beside them.

'Are you ready to——?' She broke off as she found herself looking into Hunter Scott's face. He looked as startled as she was, but typically he recovered himself first.

'Well, hello. If it isn't the opposition!' His brows were raised sardonically. 'What are you doing here?'

'What does it look like?' demanded Gussie rudely. She was ruffled by the way her body had flared in reaction to him, and promptly forgot how tempted she had been to like him when he had insisted on her having the chocolate.

'It *looks* like you're a waitress, but I got the impression that your every waking moment was devoted to saving the earth from despoilers like myself?' His mockery was all too familiar, and Gussie set her teeth. She was *not* going to let him rile her.

'I have to support myself somehow. Actually,' she went on boldly, 'I'm surprised to see *you* here. I'd have thought you would turn up your nose at anything less than a four-star restaurant.'

That infuriatingly amused look was back in his eyes. 'Well, there we are. It just goes to show that you should never judge people on first impressions, doesn't it? I happen to be rather bored with four-star restaurants so we thought we'd try somewhere different. We were told this place had good, unpretentious food, a warm atmosphere and——' he hesitated significantly '—charming service.'

Gussie tightened her lips, but Hunter continued smoothly before she had a chance to reply. 'Frances, this is Gussie Blake.'

For the first time Gussie realised that Hunter had a companion, an elegantly dressed woman of about his own age. Frances had a smooth cap of dark hair, perfect features and green eyes that were surveying Gussie coldly. In the face of such alarming sophistication, Gussie immediately felt gauche and somehow shabby.

'I knew Gussie's father very well in the Middle East,' Hunter was saying. 'Gussie, this is Frances Tyler.'

The two women acknowledged the introduction without enthusiasm. Frances gave a rather bored nod and was clearly wondering why Hunter was bothering with a mere waitress.

'Frances is my PR director,' Hunter explained with an ironic gleam. 'So she'll be working closely with me on the Whin Farm project.'

'Really?' said Gussie between her teeth. 'I hope you've told her not to expect an easy ride?'

Frances raised an eyebrow and sent Hunter an enquiring look. 'I have to admit that I haven't got round

to warning her about the terrible threat posed by you
and your friends yet,' he said with such sarcasm that
Gussie longed to haul out and hit him. So he didn't even
think Future Green's protests were worth mentioning to
his PR director? He would soon find out how wrong he
was to dismiss them quite that easily!

Her stormy eyes met his in unspoken defiance. 'Are
you ready to order?' she said with commendable
restraint.

Hunter sat back in his chair and grinned wickedly up
at her. He was clearly enjoying the fact that she couldn't
argue with a customer. 'Well...what do you
recommend?'

'The vegetarian moussaka is very good.'

Frances shuddered at the thought. 'No cranky vegetarian dishes for me, thank you! I'll have the grilled
sole and a green salad. No dressing.' She didn't even
bother to look at Gussie as she ordered.

'And I'll have the steak, please,' said Hunter, snapping
his menu shut and handing it to Gussie with a pro-
vocative smile. 'If you can bear to serve such a carni-
vorous meal!'

She was sure he had chosen it deliberately to annoy.
'How would you like it cooked?' she asked, refusing to
rise to the bait.

'Rare,' he said. Of course.

'With raw blood,' Gussie said as if to herself, scribbling down the order. 'Would you like a knife and fork,
or would you prefer to tear at it with your teeth?'

Frances looked shocked, but Hunter met Gussie's look
appreciatively. 'A knife and fork, please. I'm feeling

civilised tonight. Are we allowed wine or must it be organic mead?'

Gussie clenched her fingers around her pen. 'There's
a wine-list on the table,' she said between her teeth.

'So there is.' Hunter flicked through it. 'As Frances
is having fish, we'll have a bottle of that Australian
Chardonnay.'

'Fine.' Gussie practically snatched the wine-list out of
his hand, and stalked off. She kicked open the kitchen
door, slammed the order on to the counter and then
banged her order book down on the bar so hard that
Tony jumped.

'A bottle of Australian Chardonnay,' she said tightly.

'Coming up.' Tony looked at her curiously. 'Who is
that guy? You were talking to him for ages.'

'That,' said Gussie with emphasis, 'is Hunter Scott.'

'Ah! The demon developer himself?'

'The very same.'

Tony pulled a bottle out of the fridge and checked the
label before reaching for the corkscrew. 'Is that his wife
with him?' He couldn't bear not to know who everybody
was.

Gussie glanced morosely over her shoulder. She could
just see Frances leaning forward and laughing with
Hunter. Probably sneering at the thought of Future
Green's opposition, Gussie thought, still smarting at
Hunter's dismissive attitude. 'Not yet, but she's working
on it.'

Tony grinned. 'Miaow! It's not like you to be catty,
Gussie! Fancy him yourself, do you?'

'Don't be ridiculous!'

'He's not really your type, I suppose,' Tony decided reluctantly, studying Hunter in a covert way. 'A bit too tough and successful for you. You prefer lame ducks, don't you?'

'What do you mean?' Gussie asked grumpily.

'Well, take Simon Mansfield, for instance.'

'Simon's not a lame duck!'

'He's not exactly successful either, though, is he?' Tony had met Simon on several occasions and made no secret of the fact that he disliked him quite as much as Simon despised him.

'Yes, he is!' she protested. 'He runs Future Green practically single-handed.'

'What's so great about that? If he's so successful, why didn't he stay in that job in London he's always boasting about?' The cork came out of the bottle with a satisfying sound and Tony set the bottle on the bar while he rummaged for an ice-bucket. 'If you ask me, he couldn't cope with it. People like Simon like to make a big noise and they can only do that in a little pond like Bracklewick. That Hunter Scott, now, you can tell he doesn't need to make a noise at all, but he'd make himself heard no matter how big the pool was.'

'You can tell all that just by handing him a menu?' marvelled Gussie with sarcasm.

'We had a bit of chat as I showed them to their table. He seems a nice bloke. At least he's got a sense of humour, which is more than you can say for your precious Simon.'

Gussie didn't deign to reply. She took the ice-bucket, plonked in the bottle and marched over to Hunter's table where she set it down with a sharp click. Simon was right about Tony, she thought furiously, forgetting for a moment how often she and Tony giggled together and how, in spite of his cynicism, he always let her have time off when she needed it.

Her lips pressed together angrily, she poured some wine into Hunter's glass and waited for him to taste it. Customer or not, she was determined not to say another word to him, but, infuriatingly, Hunter merely nodded and carried on talking to Frances.

Balked of her opportunity to show him that she was ignoring him, Gussie spent the rest of the evening in a bad mood. She tried not to watch Hunter, but his smile kept catching at the corner of her eye. Fortunately, Jane dealt with their meals, so she had no need to go near them, but, even so, she was annoyingly aware of the way Hunter lifted his glass and laughed and smiled across at Frances.

She *was* attractive, Gussie acknowledged grudgingly. The cold look that had inspected Gussie so thoroughly had vanished, and she was obviously a charming companion. Hunter had introduced her as a colleague, but you didn't smile at colleagues in quite that intimate way, thought Gussie, deciding that Frances must have replaced the Imogen her father had remembered so admiringly. Hunter evidently liked his women smart and successful and sophisticated. Gussie told herself that she didn't care, she was just surprised that he had bothered to kiss the wet, grubby and patently unsophisticated girl she had been yesterday.

As always, her stomach clenched at the memory and she turned away. It had been a brief, calculating kiss and the Imogens and Franceses of this world would laugh at the way the mere memory was enough to set her senses reeling.

Jane was very impressed by Hunter. She came up behind Gussie as she was trying not to watch him help Frances into her jacket and walk towards the door. 'He's gorgeous, isn't he?'

'Who?' said Gussie, hastily gathering cutlery to reset one of the empty tables.

'Table two. You took their order, didn't you?'

'Yes,' Gussie said unwillingly.

'Did you notice what a lovely smile he had? I came over all funny whenever I looked at him! But you could tell he was *somebody*.'

'Could you?' said Gussie coldly.

Jane began sorting out the condiments. 'He had a sort of presence, you know. Charisma. He was nice, too.'

'I didn't notice,' Gussie snapped and went off to lay tables and wish people would stop telling her how marvellous Hunter was. That swift smile of his wouldn't be much consolation to the animals and birds driven out of the woods or the hedgerows bulldozed out of the way when he came to build his leisure centre!

She had told Simon that she could deal with Hunter Scott by herself, but he seemed no more likely to listen to her now than he had before. She pondered the problem overnight, and decided to ask her father's advice the next morning on the grounds of knowing your enemy was halfway to defeating him.

'Hunter?' said her father, when tackled over the breakfast table. 'Now there's a man who's going to go far. You don't want to let that charm fool you. He can be very tough indeed when required.'

Gussie refrained from pointing out that Hunter hadn't bothered to waste much of his charm on her and that she was far from underestimating his toughness. 'What would be the best way to approach him?'

'Honestly,' John Blake said without hesitation. 'He's no fool and he won't waste time with any nonsense, but if you've got a reasonable point of view he'll listen. I was working for the opposition, as it were, in the Gulf, but I always found him fair and scrupulously honest in all his dealings.' He paused and eyed his daughter with resignation. 'I presume this is about Whin Farm?'

'Well ... yes.'

'I wouldn't bother threatening him in that case.'

Faint colour tinged Gussie's cheeks as she remembered what had happened the last time she had threatened Hunter. If only she could get that wretched kiss out of her mind!

'You can shout and scream all you like,' her father went on. 'It won't bother Hunter. If you must have your say, I would go to him and put your objections to him quietly and sensibly, without the hysterical slogans that your friend Simon Mansfield is so keen on.'

'But he's not going to change his mind just because of anything I say,' Gussie said desperately.

'He might do. At least you'll have tried.'

Gussie turned his words over in her mind as she cycled into Bracklewick. The sun was shining and her spirits rose as she free-wheeled down the last hill into the town. This was her chance to prove to Hunter that she couldn't be dismissed quite as easily as he so obviously thought! She had promised to do some shopping for her mother, but after that she would take her father's advice and tackle Hunter again.

This time, though, she would be calm, collected, and show him that she was able to put their previous unfortunate meetings behind her. He wasn't a man to be moved by sentiment or passionate arguments, and for the sake of Whin Farm she had to persuade him to change his plans. So this time he would see a different Gussie, someone as cool and reasoned as he was. So impressed would he be by her persuasive arguments that he would decide forthwith to cancel all his plans for the leisure complex.

This daydream left Gussie feeling rather guilty about Jack Wilson, and she had to extend it to incorporate Hunter, in a fit of newly converted zeal, buying the land to let it run wild without interference from man.

All she had to do was find Hunter. As it turned out, this was easier than she thought, although their meeting didn't get off to quite the start she had anticipated when she literally bumped into him coming out of the supermarket. She wasn't looking where she was going, her attention riveted on balancing all her shopping in her arms, and her mind pondering how she would begin her speech to Hunter. Her first thought as she collided with a rock-hard body was for her fruit.

'Oh, my oranges!' she cried, grabbing at them as they fell, and losing her precarious grip on everything else in the process. The whole lot tumbled down on to the pavement and she dived down to retrieve them. An orange rolled across the pavement into the gutter.

'I'm so sorry!' The man squatted down to help her as she scrabbled for her purchases, and as they glanced at each other, nose to nose, both recoiled in surprise. The piece of cheese Gussie had just picked up dropped unnoticed from her hand as she stared at Hunter Scott.

'You!'

'How very dramatic,' he said sardonically. His face was very close. She could see the creases around his eyes and the firm texture of his skin.

'I might have known it would be you!' she said with some bitterness, wondering if she would ever get used to the way her heart jumped whenever she saw him. So much for her plans to impress him with her coolness and competence! It was somehow typical of him to thwart her by finding her crawling around the pavement in this undignified way.

Hunter began collecting the oranges which had rolled out of their paper bag. 'I might say the same thing,' he said in a resigned voice. 'Our paths seem doomed to cross—literally in this case. Do you always wander around the streets without looking where you're going?'

Gussie's face was flaming with embarrassment. She knew the collision had been her fault, but it didn't make it any easier to hear it from Hunter. 'I was thinking,' she said gruffly.

'I don't want to discourage you from such a promising activity, but I wish you'd confine your thinking to quiet, secluded places,' he said with some acidity. 'Preferably well away from roads and pavements. It would be a lot easier on my nerves. That's twice I've nearly mown you down, and you might not be quite so lucky a third time.'

Gussie bit back an angry retort just in time. She stood a fat chance of impressing him now, but there was no point in making things worse. She could still try and make him listen to her. She struggled to regain her composure as she gathered her scattered shopping together and piled it into her arms.

Hunter watched her with an exasperated expression. 'It's just a suggestion,' he said, retrieving the last orange from the gutter, 'but wouldn't it have been a good idea to have put all this in a carrier bag?'

'They've only got plastic ones in the shop,' Gussie explained, sitting back on her heels. Her cheeks were still pink, but her eyes were bright and clear. 'They end up blowing around the country and the animals choke on them. I told the shop they ought to provide bags that could be recycled, like the brown paper ones, but the girl on the till just looked at me as if I were a nutter.'

'You amaze me,' said Hunter drily.

Gussie saw the glint in his eyes. 'These things make a difference,' she said, instantly on the defensive.

'I'm sure you're right.' He glanced down at the tin in his hand. 'I'm just surprised that you're buying tins at all...oh, I see, it's tuna caught with dolphin-friendly nets. Just as well!'

Gussie bristled. 'They're for my mother.'

'That's what they all say.' He watched her as she staggered to her feet, eyeing her battered shopping with some dismay, and shook his head.

'Here, give me some of that,' he offered irritably, relieving her of half her burden. 'I don't know why you have to make life so difficult for yourself. One plastic bag isn't going to spell the end of the world.'

'It's the principle,' said Gussie, flushing, and he sighed.

'Spare me the lecture, please! It's too early for principles. I'm more concerned with practicalities, like what you're planning to do with this stuff. Where are you going?'

Gussie hesitated. It didn't look as if he was going to be in any mood to listen to her, but she might not get another chance. 'Actually, I was on my way to your office,' she said at last.

'You were?' He raised an eyebrow. 'Now I really *am* surprised! I thought from the way you handed over our table last night to your charming colleague that you wanted as little to do with me as possible?'

Gussie looked a little hunted. She had hoped he wouldn't refer to her rudeness in the wine bar. 'Yes, well, I've been thinking, and I rather hoped I could arrange a time to come and talk to you.'

'What about? Or can I guess?'

'You can probably guess,' she said. Her father had said there was no point in being anything less than honest. 'It's about Whin Farm. But I don't want to lecture you or harangue you,' she hurried on. 'I just want...to talk to you.'

Hunter looked down into her pleading eyes. The sunshine caught them, turning them into a blaze of amber. 'All right,' he said slowly. 'Come along and talk to me now.'

'Now?' she faltered.

'Why not? I presume your services aren't required in the wine bar just yet?'

She hadn't had time to prepare her speech, but Gussie decided that she might as well seize the opportunity while she had it.

'The office is just behind the market-place,' Hunter said, setting off as if he took her assent for granted.

Gussie trotted along beside him. He had a long, easy stride and she thought they must look an odd couple, both carrying an armful of assorted shopping but otherwise completely different. He was dark and decisive, she was pink-cheeked and scruffy. He wore a grey suit that emphasised his air of strength and authority, she hurried after him in the inevitable jeans and faded shirt. He looked like what he was, a successful businessman, and she had only a muddled sense of right and wrong.

It was funny that when he kissed her none of those differences seemed to matter.

Don't think about the kiss, she reminded herself frantically. Think about Whin Farm and how important it is.

'We're still a little bare,' said Hunter, unlocking the door and showing her into a bright room containing three desks. An enlarged map of Whin Farm was the only decoration. 'The rest of the stuff arrives from London next week.'

He deposited Gussie's shopping on a chair, and she followed his example. Even without the usual office paraphernalia, the room exuded professionalism. She hadn't realised quite how advanced the plans for Whin Farm were.

'Are you planning on having a permanent office?' she asked nervously.

'That's right.' Hunter glanced at her face as she studied the map on the wall. 'We don't want to hide anything. As long as we're building, the public will be able to come in here and ask questions and see our designs for the project.' He paused and then said coolly, 'So you see, we're here to stay.'

'Oh.' Gussie chewed her lip. She was obviously wasting her time here, and she half expected Hunter to tell her that she might as well go, but instead he offered her a coffee.

'I'm afraid we haven't got any herb teas in stock!' he said and Gussie gritted her teeth. He was making fun of her again.

'Coffee will do fine, thank you,' she said stiffly.

Hunter disappeared into a galley kitchen, but re-appeared a couple of minutes later with two steaming mugs of coffee. He gestured Gussie towards a chair before he handed her one, and then settled himself behind his desk. He had taken off his jacket, and now rolled up his sleeves and loosened his tie, but in spite of his casual appearance his eyes were sharp and clever.

'What was it you wanted to say?' he asked at last as she hesitated.

He sat easily in his chair, but Gussie sensed the hidden steel in him. He was dark and remote behind his desk and she looked at him as if he were a stranger. The lines of his face were cool and decisive and there was a ruthless set to jaw and mouth that sent a shiver of awareness down her spine, reminding her that here was a man used to getting his own way. He was a hard-headed businessman; she must have been mad to think that she could persuade him to change his mind.

'Well?' Hunter prompted impatiently.

Gussie swallowed. Now that she was here, she might as well have her say, even if it wasn't going to do any good.

'I wanted to apologise, first of all, for the demonstration at Whin Farm the other evening. I've been thinking about it, and I realise that that's not the way to go about things. That doesn't mean we don't feel just as strongly about Whin Farm.' The slate-blue eyes watching her were shuttered, and it was impossible to gauge his reaction.

She hesitated, wondering how to go on. 'Won't you please reconsider your plans?' she pleaded at last. All she could do was say what she felt. 'Some of the trees in Whin Woods have been growing there for four hundred years, the older hedgerows almost as long. They can't be replaced. It takes centuries to create a wood like the one up there, and there are so few undisturbed areas left. We *must* preserve them. They're . . . they're part of our heritage. They've been here so much longer than we have, and they deserve a chance to survive.'

Hunter still said nothing. He sat very still, watching her with those unreadable eyes, and she jumped to her feet, unable to sit beneath his gaze any longer. 'It's not just a question of a few trees or hedges,' she went on, pacing around the office, clenching and unclenching her hands. She was very conscious of his eyes following her, and struggled to keep her mind on Whin Farm.

'They support a whole cycle of life: plants and animals and birds and insects. If you take one away, the others will die too. Badgers aren't the only creatures who'll be disturbed if you tamper with the woods. I know you think I'm being sentimental, but who will talk for them if we don't? There are so many other creatures who live there. Who'll talk for the owl or the frog or the chaffinch or the vole or the poor humble beetle? They're not very glamorous, but they have a right to live as much as we have. *Please* give them a chance and reconsider.'

She stopped suddenly as Hunter got to his feet. He was going to throw her out, tell her to stop wasting his time. Gussie's shoulders slumped. She had made a mess of it. Instead of the cool reasoning she had promised, she had been carried away by emotion as usual. The trouble was that she just didn't know how to argue any other way.

Well, she had done her best. Now it was up to Simon to lead the fight for Whin Farm.

'Where are you going?' Hunter demanded as she turned for the door.

'I didn't expect you to change your mind,' she muttered. 'It was good of you to listen.'

'Then why don't *you* listen to what *I've* got to say for once?'

Gussie braced herself for a scathing review of her arguments. 'Very well.'

'In spite of all that muddled sentimentality,' Hunter said, 'I'm prepared to do what you ask.'

CHAPTER FIVE

'YOU are?' For a moment, Gussie could only goggle at him, taken aback by such an unexpected victory, but as his words sank in a smile of vivid delight swept across her face. 'You mean you won't develop Whin Farm after all?' she said eagerly.

'I don't mean anything of the kind,' Hunter said in a crisp voice and her face fell ludicrously.

'But you just said——'

'I said I would do what you asked, and what you asked me to do was reconsider. That means I'm prepared to look at my plans again in the light of what you've told me. It doesn't mean I'm going to change my mind about the development. I've bought the land, and I'm not going to back out of the deal I've agreed with Jack Wilson now. Too many jobs depend on it.'

'And too many profits?' Gussie suggested, bitter disappointment sharpening her tongue. For one glorious moment she had thought that she had saved Whin Farm, but she should have known better. Hunter Scott wasn't going to be influenced by anything *she* said.

Hunter's mouth thinned disapprovingly. 'Yes, profits, too. I've got a business to run, not a charity. I can't afford to indulge in the sort of sentimentality you go in for.'

'Then there isn't any point in my wasting any more of your time, is there?' she said, struggling to control her disappointment. Turning on her heel, she headed for the door again, only to find herself brought up short by his hand, which shot out and grasped her arm in a grip of iron.

He swung her round to face him once more. 'Don't be in such a hurry! For someone supposedly so in tune with the slower rhythms of nature you're far too quick to jump to conclusions, Gussie. I haven't finished yet.'

Gussie could feel his fingers burning through the thin cotton of her sleeve. The sheer momentum as he swung her round had brought her back close to him, and she was overwhelmed by the solid, steely power of his body. Awareness caught at her throat and she stared desperately at his tie, unable to meet his eyes in case he saw the memory of that brief kiss they had shared shimmering in her own like a shameful, exciting secret.

'You can at least do me the courtesy of hearing me out,' Hunter went on, propelling her across the room and pushing her down into the chair. Gussie sat rubbing her arm where he had held her and watched resentfully as he resumed his seat and leant forward, resting his linked hands on the desk.

'Now,' he said. 'I suggest you listen, and then *think* before you say anything.' Gussie, who had just opened her mouth to speak, shut it abruptly. 'I'm not going to change my mind about the development at Whin Farm, so you might as well accept that. However, I *am* prepared to reconsider how the project is designed and managed. In spite of what you obviously believe, I'm just as concerned as you are to preserve the countryside. In fact, it's in my interests to be concerned. Not only does the success of the project depend on it being in

unspoilt country, but people are also much more aware
of green issues. Not many take their concern to the ex-
tremes that you do, but if we make the project as environment-friendly as possible that will be a selling point
for us.'

He looked across the desk at Gussie who was listening
with evident suspicion. 'That's where you come in. I'm
offering you a place on the team as an environmental
consultant.'

Gussie's jaw dropped. 'A consultant? Me?'

'Why not?' he said coolly. 'As long as you're prepared to accept that this project is going to go ahead
anyway, you could be in a position to ensure that we do
as little damage to the environment as possible. We might
even be able to do some good with your advice. For
instance, if plastic bags really are the hazard you claim
them to be, we could agree that only recyclable paper
ones will be used on the site.'

Sitting back in his chair, he linked his hands behind
his head and regarded her speculatively. 'You don't seem
very enthusiastic about the idea. I'd have thought you
would jump at the chance of doing something constructive about what you believe instead of just protesting wildly to no effect.'

'Who says it's to no effect?' Gussie said, looking bale-
fully back at him.

'I do. Come on, Gussie, admit it. Waving a few placards around isn't going to change anything. I'm offering
you a real opportunity to put your view forward and all
you can do is sit there and look suspicious!'

'Perhaps I'm not convinced that you'll really listen,'
she said, still wary of his motives. 'How do I know you're

not just trying to get me on your side as a way of stopping Future Green's protests?'

Hunter sat forward again, bringing his hands back down on to the desk with a smack that made Gussie flinch. 'Frankly, Augusta, Future Green aren't that much of a threat. I dare say you can be annoying when you try, but you haven't got the organisation or the resources to be anything more than a mild irritant.'

'If you think that, why are you offering to make me a consultant?'

'Because I think you're rather different from the others in Future Green. You know the area well, and you obviously care passionately about it.'

Unbidden, the memory of his words before he kissed her came back to Gussie. *There are much better things to care passionately about than the environment.*

'Also,' he went on with a touch of humour, 'you're clearly not going to go away, so I may as well give you something useful to do instead of getting in the way. At least then I'd know where you are instead of wondering when you're going to leap out in front of me!'

There was that disquieting gleam in his eyes again. Gussie's amber gaze slid away from his. He was laughing at her. Did he honestly think he could win her over by offering her a job, just like offering sweets to a child? Working with a property developer would mean betraying everything Future Green stood for. She ought to tell him just what he could do with his 'consultancy'... but would that be the best thing for Whin Farm?

Throwing his offer back in his face would be immensely satisfying, but it would leave her back at square one. Future Green would have lost a perfect opportunity to exert some influence. Looking at that mocking glint in his eyes, Gussie didn't believe for one moment that Hunter would take the slightest notice of anything she said, but if she joined his team he could hardly refuse to let her have her say. More importantly, it would give her an ideal opportunity to find out exactly what his plans were. She could report back to Future Green; once armed with the facts they would be in a far stronger position to oppose the development.

'I'm delighted to see that you've taken my advice to think before you speak,' said Hunter drily, 'but I haven't got all day. It doesn't take all that long to decide whether you want a job or not.'

'I've got a job,' Gussie pointed out. 'I can't let Tony down.'

'This wouldn't be a full-time job. I suggest you come in in the mornings and look at the plans—the real plans, not the ones you and your friends claim to have seen—and then you can tell us what can be improved or changed to help the environment.'

'Would you really listen to me?' she asked sceptically.

'If you've got a good point to make.' Hunter leant back and stuck his hands in his pockets. 'I'm not interested in any hare-brained schemes to provide rest homes for hedgehogs or anything like that, but it's in my own interests to have things as "green" as possible. If people think I've been wantonly destructive, they won't support the project. I have to admit that I'd already considered getting a professional consultant on the environment to look at our plans, but I don't see why you shouldn't do the job just as well.'

'And so much more cheaply,' Gussie said with un-characteristic sharpness, but Hunter only smiled, that swift, disconcerting smile that clutched at the base of her spine.

'For someone so sentimental, you can be positively cynical, Gussie,' he said, shaking his head in reproof. 'You'll just have to believe me when I say that saving money was not my reason for offering you the job, but since we're talking about money, do you want to charge a fee, or would you rather have a salary?'

Gussie looked blankly at him. 'You mean you'd pay me?'

'Of course. You don't think I'd ask you to work for nothing, do you?'

'I don't need any money,' she said quickly, afraid that he would misunderstand her. If she was going to spy for Future Green, she couldn't possibly accept any money from him. That really would go against all her principles.

'A struggling waitress, and you don't need any money?' Hunter raised an eyebrow in polite disbelief, but Gussie's clear eyes met his squarely.

'If I can influence your plans for Whin Farm, that will be enough for me.'

'So you'll accept the job, then?' he said briskly, catching Gussie off balance.

'Well . . . y-yes, I suppose so,' she stammered. What had she done?

'Good.' Hunter pushed back his chair and stood up. 'What time do you have to be at the wine bar?'

'Twelve o'clock,' said Gussie, flustered by the sudden change of subject.

'In that case, I suggest I take you out to Whin Farm now and show you exactly what I'm planning to do. There's no point in your making any suggestions until you know that, and the information you have at Future Green seems to be sadly misleading.'

Before she had gathered herself together and thought of a reason to protest, Gussie found herself borne outside and installed in the big black car that she remembered so well. Hunter was giving her no opportunity to change her mind, she realised, and she eyed him uncertainly. It was hard to believe that he really considered her opinion worth having, but why then should he be so keen to offer her a job? Gussie decided that her first reaction had been the right one. However much Hunter might pooh-pooh the idea, it would make sense for him to keep her under his eye where she couldn't get up to any mischief that might damage the Whin Farm project.

Snapping her seatbelt into place as if she was girding herself for battle, Gussie tilted her chin in unconscious defiance. If Hunter Scott thought she was that easily taken in, he had another think coming. She would use him just as he was using her.

As the car powered up the hill out of the town, she determined to remain cool and distant to show Hunter that even if he *had* managed to get his own way this time he couldn't take her for granted. Unfortunately, he seemed equally aloof and happy to concentrate on driving.

Gussie tried not to look at him, but her eyes kept skittering towards his mouth. Did he remember that kiss that glowed so persistently at the edge of her mind? Had he lain awake trying to still his racing heart while he pushed the memory aside? Did his spine tingle at the mere thought of her mouth?

She didn't think so.

'You're very quiet,' said Hunter, glancing at her. 'Afraid one of your Future Green friends will see you in a car?'

'No.' Gussie pulled herself together. She wondered what he would say if she told him the truth. 'I was just wondering where Frances was,' she improvised. For the first time she wondered if Frances's job was as meaningless as her own, an excuse for Hunter to have her around but for quite different reasons, but Hunter's reply seemed to indicate that Frances at least had a real job.

'She's gone off to chat up the local television stations. With any luck we'll get some good coverage to explain what we're going to do at Whin Farm before people get the wrong idea, like you and your protesting friends.'

'You haven't convinced me yet that we *have* got the wrong idea,' Gussie pointed out sharply. He needn't think that she was going to take everything at *his* say-so!

'That's what I'm about to do,' Hunter said calmly.

Gussie immediately resolved to remain unconvinced, if only to spite him, but as Hunter showed her round the site she found it increasingly hard to maintain her hostility.

'We'll use the existing farmhouse and steadings for the restaurant and bar,' he explained as they strolled into the farmyard. He gestured towards the stables. 'This will be where people arrive, so there'll be a reception point and exhibition area over there. All the buildings will be in local stone so that it's all in character.'

'I suppose the multi-storey car park is going to be "in character" too?' Gussie said waspishly, refusing to be impressed. She had been horrified when Simon had told everyone at Future Green about the number of cars the Whin Farm leisure complex was likely to attract. Nothing less than a multi-storey car park would accommodate them all, he'd said.

Hunter looked resigned. 'That smacks suspiciously of Future Green's immaculate research into the supposed facts! I've got no intention of putting up a multi-storey car park, even if I could get planning permission to build one out here, which is, I can tell you, extremely unlikely. Here, I'll show you where the car parks will be.'

Taking her arm, he led her back to the track and pointed out a rubbly field near the road. 'People will have to leave their cars there and walk down to the centre. As you can see, it's not land that can be used for anything else; there are no rare wild flowers growing there and we'll plant trees to hide as much of the cars as possible.' He glanced down at her mutinous face. 'Satisfied?'

Gussie folded her arms and searched for an objection, but it was hard to argue with planting trees. She had to content herself with what she hoped was an enigmatic look as Hunter pointed out areas for the various sporting facilities, all built in stone and separated by land that would be left to grow naturally.

'I don't like the manicured effect,' he said as they walked around the edge of a field. 'The whole point is that people should feel as if they're in the country, not in a park. The grounds will need a certain amount of care, of course, but I want them to look as wild as possible. We'll sow wild flowers and plant trees, but I hope it won't look as artificial as it in fact is. We don't want people trampling all over the flowers, so we'll have to put in paths, but we'll lay down bark instead of concrete.'

Gussie nodded reluctant approval. At this rate she wouldn't be able to find anything to criticise! The reality of the plans that Hunter had shown her were a far cry from Future Green's impression. It should have re-assured her, but all she could feel was cross that Hunter had been proved right.

'Access to the woods and the moors will be a major part of the centre's attraction,' Hunter said as he held a dilapidated gate open for Gussie and they crossed the road into the cool shade of the woods. 'Let's hear your opinion, Gussie. What do you think we should do with the woods?'

'Absolutely nothing,' she said with a snap. These woods had been her refuge for as long as she could re-member and she couldn't bear to think of them being cut down to make room for more facilities, that horrible word. 'What were you planning? Log cabins? Mountain-bike trails? Your-chance-to-be-a-lumberjack compe-titions?' She ducked angrily beneath an overhanging branch. 'You might as well give all the wildlife notice to move out now!'

'Now just a minute.' Hunter caught her up easily and hauled her round to face him, and with a sickening sense of shock Gussie realised that he was very angry. 'I can't decide whether you're pigheaded or stupid, or both,' he said in a quiet voice that sent a chill down Gussie's spine. 'I've tolerated your sweeping generalisations about what

I'm supposed to be doing here, based on nothing more
than hearsay, because I thought that you really believed
what you were saying. Stupidly, I assumed that if I could
show you what was really going to happen you would
realise that the centre would benefit the environment,
not destroy it. But no! You're so determined to paint
me as the villain of the piece that you won't admit that
you've been wrong. Has anything I've shown you or said
to you so far suggested that I'm likely to build log cabins
or hold tree-felling competitions in these woods?' His
fingers tightened around her arms as he shook her. '*Has*
it?'

Shocked out of her own anger by the fury in his expression, Gussie stared up at him with huge amber eyes.
'N-no.'

'Do you really think this centre is going to be the environmental disaster you and Future Green claim it to
be?' he demanded. 'Because if you do after all I've shown
you, we may as well go back to Bracklewick right now!'
He let her go with an exclamation of disgust, and Gussie
held her arms defensively, rubbing her arms where his
fingers had dug into her skin.

'No, I don't think that.' Her knees were shaking. She
supposed she ought to feel pleased that she had provoked him out of his rather mocking detachment, but
all she felt was scared and very, very small. He was right.
She *had* been determined to think the worst of him. 'It's
just...' She looked at the massive beech that stretched
its branches over the narrow path. 'It's just that I wish
things wouldn't change. I used to come to the woods a
lot when I was a child. There was never anyone else here;
I don't think Jack Wilson has been near them for years.'

She shrugged, half embarrassed, but wanting him to understand. 'I always thought of them as mine. When I heard that you'd bought the woods and were planning to turn them into a leisure centre, I felt as if someone had come trampling into my home.' She couldn't meet his eyes. 'I know it's selfish, but it's how I feel.'

There was a silence, then Hunter reached out with a rueful smile and lifted a lock of her hair. He rubbed it between his fingers almost absently as he looked down at her. 'I'm glad you told me,' he said at last. 'I was beginning to think that you were as blinkered by ideology as your friends at Future Green, but this is a more personal battle for you, isn't it, Gussie?'

She nodded, surprised at the gentle note in his voice. She hadn't expected him to be so understanding. 'It's not that I wouldn't fight for any threatened countryside, but these woods are special.' She was achingly aware of his closeness and the feel of his fingers in her hair.

'I can't promise things won't change,' Hunter said, dropping his hand. 'But you can help ensure that any damage to the environment is minimal, and I can promise that the most that will happen in these woods is some clearing to let the trees grow, and a few paths. Those badgers of yours won't even know we're here!'

Gussie risked a glance at him. He was smiling, but the mockery had gone, and she felt a dangerous glow of warmth light deep inside her.

'Really?' she said.

'Really,' he confirmed solemnly. 'I'm sorry I shouted at you, Gussie.'

She flushed. 'I deserved it. I *was* being pigheaded. I was just cross because I couldn't find anything to criticise.'

'I'm sure you'll think of something,' Hunter said, but the glint in his eyes was teasing rather than exasperated. He looked around him with pleasure. 'I haven't had a chance to explore the woods much. Why don't you lead the way?'

So Gussie took him down narrow, overgrown paths until they came to a clearing where the sun filtered through the leaves. It was very quiet and a still, secretive calm hung on the air.

'You certainly know your way around these woods,' Hunter said. 'I'd never have been able to find my way here.'

'Good,' said Gussie. 'This is the badgers' set and the fewer people who can find it the better.'

Squatting, she traced some vertical scoring on a tree-trunk with her finger. 'There are still badgers around, too. Look, this is where they stand on their back legs and sharpen their claws on the bark.'

'How do you know so much about them?' he asked, watching her with a strange expression in his eyes.

'I used to come here and watch them a lot. I even built a hide.' She pointed up into the spreading branches of an oak tree where a few planks rested precariously. 'There it is up there. There used to be a bit more camouflage, of course, but it's downwind of the set so if I lay still long enough I could see the cubs come out and play.'

'It looks a little unstable,' Hunter commented with a disparaging glance upwards.

'It's perfectly safe,' she bristled, and to prove her point climbed up into the tree with the ease of long practice and wriggled forward on her stomach to the edge of the little platform. She waved down at him triumphantly. 'See?'

Hunter peered up through the leaves. Gussie's eyes were shining and her hair tumbled forward around her vivid face. 'I stand corrected,' he said gravely. 'Can I come up?'

From where Gussie lay, he looked curiously fore-shortened. A shaft of sunlight through a break in the trees highlighted the forceful lines of his nose and cheek but left his mouth in shadow. The light burnished the dark hair and made him screw up his eyes.

He had left his jacket in the car, but he still wore his tie. The sleeves of his blue shirt were rolled up and his hands were thrust casually into his pockets. He should have looked ridiculous standing in the middle of a wood in his office clothes, but somehow he didn't. Gussie had the feeling that Hunter Scott would never look ridiculous.

'It's rather grubby,' she said doubtfully, thinking of his suit.

'That doesn't matter. What are dry-cleaners for?'

Hunter had climbed a few trees in his youth too, she decided, watching the agile way he climbed up to join her. She brushed the debris off the platform so that he could stretch out beside her and they lay side by side, squinting down into the dappled shade of the clearing. There was little activity in the broad daylight, but a jay alighted on a nearby branch and regarded them with a puzzled air before flying off again.

'It's very peaceful,' he said. 'I can see why you wanted to keep it to yourself.'

'I used to spend hours up here, just watching and waiting,' she said, picking an oak leaf from the platform and letting it drop over the edge. They both watched it spiral slowly down into the clearing. 'Whenever I felt miserable I'd come here and lie in the quiet and feel better.'

'Did you often feel miserable?'

Gussie propped her chin in her hands and considered. 'No more than any other adolescent, I suppose. I was a rather solitary child and never really fitted in at school. I was never particularly interested in boys or pop stars, and everyone thought I was rather strange for preferring the woods to standing around the walls at discos.'

'Were the boys interested in you?' She could feel his eyes on her face, unaware of how the dappled sunlight gave her the fey, elusive look of a wild animal.

'Not really. I don't think they ever knew what to say to me, and I certainly never knew what to say to them. I was much more comfortable with the badgers!'

'Lucky badgers.' There was an odd note in Hunter's voice and Gussie glanced at him curiously, but he was looking down at the set and she could reading nothing in his face but polite interest.

Suddenly she was overcome with embarrassment. Why was she telling him all this? He wasn't interested in an awkward adolescent who couldn't talk to boys. Why had she brought him here at all? This hide had been her secret for years. Why had she shown it to Hunter Scott, of all people?

She was very conscious of his lean strength beside her. He wasn't touching her, but he was lying so close that she could see the texture of his skin and the way the hair grew at his temples. He seemed absorbed by the scene below. Gussie found her gaze lingering on the angles of his face, on the heart-clenching set of his mouth and the pulse that beat below his ear, and she tingled with the need to lean over and touch her lips to his throat.

Horrified at the way her thoughts were leading, Gussie wrenched her eyes away. She might as well still be that shy, awkward adolescent for all the interest Hunter would have in her. She already knew what kind of women he liked—smart, sophisticated women like Frances and Imogen. In spite of herself, her gaze flickered over to him again. How hurt had he been by the break-up with Imogen? Judging by what her father had said, they had been very close, close enough to have been mistaken for man and wife. What would it be like to live with Hunter, be loved by Hunter? Did Frances know?

He turned his head at that moment and Gussie found herself staring helplessly into the deep, unreadable grey of his eyes. She wanted to look away but she was held, the breath caught in her throat, as his gaze locked with hers. They both lay very still and the only sound in the clearing was Gussie's pulse roaring in her ears, so loud that she was certain Hunter must be able to hear it.

The air seemed to tighten between them, as if it would drag them inexorably together. Gussie could feel her body tensing against the pressure, and Hunter's hand moved towards her, but the next moment he sat up abruptly.

'We'd better go,' he said. 'You don't want to be late for work.'

They walked back to the car in silence. Gussie didn't know whether to be relieved or disappointed that he had broken that strange, twanging tension between them. He might not even have felt it, she reasoned, but instinct told her that he must have been aware. Had he read the confused desire in her eyes, that aching need to touch him, or had he seen only the ungainly girl who preferred badgers to boys?

That would explain why he had moved away so quickly, she thought dismally as they drove back to Bracklewick. He must have been bored stiff. He was probably already regretting offering her a place on his team. He was very quiet, she thought, stealing a glance at his profile. His brow was creased into a frown and he looked remote and preoccupied. Perhaps he was wondering how to tell her not to bother coming into the office tomorrow after all?

Back at the office, Gussie began stacking her shopping into her arms until Hunter gave an exasperated sigh and disappeared in search of a cardboard box. 'Here, use this,' he said, thrusting the box at her. 'I can't bear to see you drop that lot again.'

Gussie was obscurely reassured by his return to a more familiar, irritable manner. 'Do you still want me to act as your consultant?' she asked shyly.

'Of course.' He looked surprised. 'I thought we'd agreed?'

Had they agreed, or had she allowed herself to be pushed into doing what he wanted? Gussie was no longer sure that it even mattered. She had gone to Whin Farm determined to find fault with Hunter's plans, but now she found that she badly wanted the job for its own sake.

'Yes,' she said, picking up the cardboard box. 'I'll tell Future Green tonight.'

Her enthusiasm grew as she served out the usual variety of quiches and salads in the wine bar. Pushing her unsettling awareness of Hunter to the back of her mind, she tried to concentrate on Whin Farm. The more she thought about it, the better she felt. The plans for the leisure complex weren't nearly as bad as they had all thought and, if Hunter really did let her have a say on environmental issues, Future Green now had a real chance to have some influence at last, without any need to resort to the kind of aggressive tactics she secretly dreaded. This was how Future Green ought to operate in the future. Environmental experts and consultants; it had a nice ring to it.

CHAPTER SIX

BUT Simon, when she told of her agreement with Hunter Scott, was horrified.

'You've done *what*?' he shouted. The Future Green meeting had been cancelled, but Gussie had persuaded him to come round to the wine bar to hear about her successful meeting with Hunter Scott after she had finished work. She had been looking forward to seeing his face when she told him how much influence Future Green were going to have, but his reaction was far from the congratulations she had anticipated.

'I've agreed to act as a consultant for Hunter on the project,' she repeated, lowering her voice. The sunny day had blown into a stormy evening and there were still a few customers lingering over their coffee, reluctant to face the rain splattering against the windows.

'Oh, it's Hunter now, is it?' Simon sneered. 'It didn't take you long to get cosy with him!'

'He's not so bad,' Gussie hissed. 'He says he wants to make Whin Farm as environment-friendly as possible.'

'Sure he does! How could you be so naïve, Gus? If it comes to a toss-up between the environment and money, money will win every time!'

'How can you possibly know that?' she demanded angrily. 'You haven't even met him.'

'I know his type,' Simon said.

The last couple were draining the last of their wine and getting to their feet. They had paid their bill some time ago, so all Gussie had to do was open the door and wish them a friendly goodnight, but it was an effort to smile. She had never dreamt Simon would react like this.

'Simon, I really think this is the best way to influence him,' she tried again, slumping on to the stool beside him and rubbing her tired eyes. 'I can find out what's really planned for Whin Farm and if there's anything we object to on environmental grounds, well, I can put our case before we have to take any other action.'

'That's hardly the point,' said Simon contemptuously.

'But surely the whole point of our protest was to ensure that Whin Farm stayed as unspoilt as possible? This is by far the best way we can do that.'

'It's better to sacrifice Whin Farm than to give in to the system and start dealing with developers,' Simon said with finality. 'We've got to make a stand against any kind of development, full stop. If we're going to start compromising as soon as a developer starts sweet-talking us, we might as well not bother!'

Gussie sat bolt upright and stared at Simon as if she couldn't believe her ears. 'You mean you're prepared to sacrifice Whin Farm for some stupid principle?'

'You're not in a very good position to start talking about principles,' he retorted unpleasantly. 'You've just got a lot of airy-fairy ideas about the country, but when it comes down to it you're ideologically unsound. Admit it, you've sold out!'

'That's not fair!'

'Oh? I suppose the mention of money never crossed his lips?'

'He did offer me a salary but——'

'I thought as much!' cried Simon before she could finish. 'You've been bought, Gus. I'm disappointed in you.' He shook his head. 'I thought at one time that we could have had something going, you know, but I can't compromise my reputation by being seen around with someone who isn't really committed to the real issues.'

'The real issues are the flowers and the trees and the wildlife at Whin Farm. They're real, Simon, not all your fine words!' Gussie's eyes blazed gold fire. 'I don't think you really care about them at all. You don't mind what happens as long as you can carry on talking and talking and talking and never *doing* anything! The environment's just an excuse for you to act the great revolutionary and stir up trouble, isn't it?' She untied her apron and threw it down on to the counter. 'Well, I don't want to waste my time with words any more. I want to do something positive for a change.'

'If that's the way you feel, there's no more to be said,' Simon said scathingly. 'You won't be any loss to Future Green, Gus. I don't suppose anyone will even be surprised to hear that you're consorting with the enemy, though they might wonder how you could be stupid enough to believe that Hunter Scott will ever listen to anything you have to say. He'll make a fool out of you, if he hasn't already!' Draining his drink, he strutted to the door. 'When you find out what developers are really like, don't bother to come crawling back to Future Green looking for a cause!'

The bell above the door tinkled angrily as he slammed it behind him and Gussie sat down abruptly on a chair. Her knuckles were white as she clenched her hands together. Angry scenes always made her feel a little sick and the muscles in her thighs trembled with the effort of keeping her legs from wobbling.

Had she sold out? She wasn't taking any money, but had she let herself be too easily swayed by that lurking, shameful physical attraction to Hunter? Gussie unclenched her hands with an effort and tried to think honestly. Simon's attack had shaken her more than she wanted to admit, and she was stricken at the thought of Future Green's disgust. After all her loyalty to the group, her patient acceptance of all the dreary tasks in aid of a higher cause, it was devastating to feel so rejected.

Wearily, Gussie pushed her hair away from her face. She badly wanted to cry, but her pride wouldn't let her. She had been right to take up Hunter's offer, no matter what had motivated it. He might well make a fool out of her, she realised dismally, but working with him was still the best way to protect the wild areas around Whin Farm, and that mattered more than what Hunter *or* Simon thought. If Future Green wouldn't get involved, she would just have to do it by herself.

Frances was less than impressed to hear that Gussie would be joining the team. Gussie's idea of dressing for an office consisted of wearing a sleeveless shirt instead of a T-shirt with her jeans, and she could see Frances looking her up and down with a pained expression at such an unprofessional attitude.

Gussie didn't care. A sleepless night had merely stiffened her resolve. As she had so many times in the past, she had marvelled that the animal world could be so much kinder and less complicated than the human one, and she was determined to do what she could to save it. Future Green's rejection had left her feeling wary of committing herself to anyone else, and she hid her hurt behind a barrier of prickly defensiveness. She wasn't going to worry about what anyone thought, she vowed, ignoring Frances's critical appraisal. As far as she was concerned, Whin Farm was all that mattered.

Hunter was on the phone when Gussie arrived, but his eyes narrowed as they rested on her tense, tired face. 'Are you all right?' he asked brusquely as he put down the receiver.

Gussie might have mistaken his look for concern if Simon's words hadn't echoed uncomfortably at the back of her mind. '*He'll make a fool out of you.*'

'I'm fine,' she said sharply.

'In that case, we may as well go.' He stood up and searched through his jacket pocket for his car keys. 'I want to go back to Whin Farm so that you can tell Frances about all the rare species we're going to protect in the meadow. It should make good material for a Press release.'

Good material for a Press release? Was that all that wild flowers meant to him?

Gussie climbed silently into the car, ceding the front seat to Frances who monopolised Hunter's attention all the way to Whin Farm. He had never pretended to be anything other than businesslike about the development, so why should she be disappointed because her presence hadn't changed his attitude overnight? It was up to her to convince him, she reminded herself, and sat up a little straighter. Instead of feeling sorry for herself, she ought to be fighting for Whin Farm's future.

Determined to impress the meadow's importance on Hunter and Frances, Gussie opened the gate and they walked down towards the stream. Last night's storm had blown itself out and left the sky a bright, high blue. A few clouds lurked without enthusiasm over the hills, but the sunshine rippled over the long grass as it waved gently in the breeze, intensifying the rioting colours of the wild flowers and edging Gussie's hair with a halo of gold.

Hunter and Frances were discussing the format of the Press release and, forgetting them for a moment, Gussie closed her eyes and turned her face up to the sun. The air was soft and sweet and she tipped back her head so that the bright hair tumbled down her back and sunshine caught the long, pure line of her throat. Unconscious of her untamed appearance, she breathed in deeply, savouring the fragrance of the meadow. Yes, this was what mattered.

'Are you still with us?' Frances asked acidly, and Gussie's eyes snapped open to find Hunter watching her with a strangely arrested expression. It was quickly masked as he turned back to Frances, but Gussie's nerves were still tingling as she crouched down in the grass to hide her confusion.

'This is ragged robin,' she said on a half-gasp. Hadn't she decided to keep herself aloof so that Hunter had no chance to make her the fool Simon had claimed her to be? It was going to be hard to cling to her self-imposed independence if the breath was going to leak out of her every time their eyes met.

She led them across the meadow, pointing out orchids and lady-smock, crane's-bill and fairy flax, hawkweed and agrimony while Frances scribbled busily in her notebook. Gussie stooped over the flowers, touching them very gently with her fingers, insensibly soothed by their delicate beauty. She was careful to avoid looking at Hunter.

'We ought to be able to get some mileage out of this,' Frances said at last. 'We could plug the "development saves ancient meadow" line, and the flowers would make a wonderful backdrop for a television report. I'll just make a few notes while I'm here...'

She bent her glossy head over her notebook and Gussie wandered over to lean on the gate leading back to the farmyard while she waited for them. There were swallows nesting in the barn, she noticed, seeing one of the birds swoop under the eaves. She watched their aerial acrobatics with pleasure until Hunter appeared beside her, and she stiffened instinctively.

'You're justifying your appointment already,' he said, resting his arms casually on the gate. 'Frances will be able to make a good Press release now that you've told her what to write about. Left to herself, she'd have had trouble telling a buttercup from a daisy!'

Gussie hated the amused affection in his voice, so unlike the exasperation he usually used when he was talking to *her*. He obviously liked the fact that Frances was a city girl.

'She seems very efficient,' she said at last, feeling some comment was called for.

'Yes, she is. I poached her from one of the multinationals at great expense, but she's been worth every penny. She knows more about PR than anyone else I know.'

'She doesn't know very much about the country,' Gussie said tartly before she could help herself. She had been appalled to find out that Frances didn't even know the basic rules of the country code.

'That's what you're here for,' Hunter reminded her coolly.

'I'm hardly likely to forget,' she snapped, stung by his subtle reproof. 'It's perfectly obvious that I'm here as a token country bumpkin!'

He raised an eyebrow at her tone. 'Is it? That's not how I think of you, I assure you.'

'Oh? How do you think of me?'

Hunter hesitated. He looked down at her face, then over to where the swallows were still swooping and diving as if in sheer joy. 'I've told you. You're here to advise on environmental matters.'

'Naming a few wild flowers hardly counts as advising,' Gussie said sharply. 'You could just as easily have brought a field guide out with you.'

There was a pause while Hunter's eyes rested thoughtfully on her taut profile. 'You seem very cross this morning, Gussie. Is anything the matter?'

'I just want you to know that I'm not going to be fobbed off with silly little jobs to keep me out of harm's way,' she said with a challenging look. 'You offered me a post as adviser, and that's what I want to do. I'm not here for you and Frances to patronise. I'm here to make sure you do as little damage as possible to this land, and I'm going to have my say, whether you like it or not!'

'Is that the official Future Green line, or is that Augusta Blake speaking?' Hunter asked and Gussie could have hit him for the undercurrent of mockery that was back in his voice. Simon had been right; he would never take her seriously.

'I'm talking for myself,' she said tersely.

'And what does Future Green say?'

Gussie averted her face. 'They don't think I should have anything to do with you.'

'But you're here anyway,' he said in a matter-of-fact voice.

'Yes.' She paused, picking the dried moss from the gate post and rubbing it between her fingers. 'I...I thought that this was my only chance of having any influence on what happened at Whin Farm. I didn't think you would take any notice of demonstrations.'

'You were right,' he said, a grim note in his voice.

'That's why I'm not going to be pushed aside.' Gussie turned back to face him squarely. Her golden eyes were very clear and direct. 'I don't know what your reasons were for offering me this job, but now that I've accepted it I'm going to make the most of it. I don't want you to think that means I'm on your side. I'm not working for Future Green or for you. As far as I'm concerned, I'm here to protect the best interests of this land, and if it means opposing you, either within your organisation or outside, then I will.'

'Is that a challenge, Gussie?'

She lifted her chin. 'Yes.'

'Well, I like challenges better than I like threats,' he said with that sudden smile. His skin had the tanned, weathered look of a man who had spent much of his life in the hot sun, and his teeth gleamed whitely in contrast. His smile emphasised the lines around his eyes and deepened the crease in his cheek as the formidable developer dissolved into an unnervingly attractive man.

Gussie felt her bones dissolve as the warmth hit her, and she clutched at the gate for support. His words reminded her only too vividly of the time he had showed her what he thought of threats, and as she met his eyes wordlessly the memory of the kiss flared between them.

'How am I going to convince you that we both want the same thing?' asked Hunter softly, without taking his eyes from her face.

Still thinking about the kiss, Gussie caught her breath, wondering if he could read her mind, but his next words brought her down to earth.

'I'm just as determined to preserve the natural assets of Whin Farm as you are.'

'I'll be convinced by what you do, not by what you say,' she said more sharply than she intended. She was still struggling to control her breathing, and her heart knocked uncomfortably against her ribs. She must stop this!

Hunter looked solemn but the smile lingered in his eyes. 'I'll remember that,' he promised, and Gussie turned abruptly away.

'I'm ready now,' Frances said brightly, coming up to them. 'Sorry to keep you waiting, but I just wanted to get my ideas in order.' She glanced from Gussie's face to Hunter's imperturbable one, and her eyes narrowed slightly. 'Shall we get out of this field? I'm sure it's very pretty, but it doesn't do much for one's shoes.'

'You're not supposed to wear expensive Italian shoes to walk around a farm,' Hunter said as they made their way back across the farmyard to the car.

'Well, you know what a town mouse I am, darling!' Frances took his arm possessively and laughed up at him, unperturbed by his teasing. She looked very attractive with her immaculate make-up and her painted nails and her dark hair shining in the sunlight. Gussie eyed her linen trousers and expensive silk top with resentment. They made a handsome couple, she thought bitterly.

Frances was making it quite clear that Hunter belonged to her. Gussie didn't know why she was bothering. She was hardly likely to prove a rival for his attentions in her jeans and faded shirt, but for the first time she wished she had something more flattering to wear. She could never hope to be as glamorous as Frances, but still, it would be nice if Hunter could see her as a woman for a change. Unconsciously, she sighed.

'I just don't feel at home in the country,' Frances was saying as she got into the car, assuming as before that she would sit in the front with Hunter. 'I must say, I can't wait till we go back to London. How much longer till your deputy takes over and we can go home?'

Gussie tried to look uninterested, but as Hunter glanced in the rear-view mirror her gaze was drawn irresistibly to his reflection, and their eyes met for one jarring moment before she turned her head quickly away.

'Another couple of months.' His answer was for Frances, but his eyes went to the mirror again. Gussie caught a quick glimpse of his reflection before she stared determinedly out of the window.

A couple of months. She felt hollow, as if all the stuffing had been punched out of her. Of course Hunter would be leaving. He wasn't the kind of man who would want to spend the rest of his life in Bracklewick, but it had never occurred to her to think ahead to the time when he would no longer be around. Suddenly, the prospect seemed unaccountably bleak.

Gussie clutched her hands together in her lap. It shouldn't matter to her. He was just a developer, after all. The only thing they had in common was Whin Farm, and she was only interested in him in so far as he affected what happened there. She had been perfectly happy before Hunter Scott burst into her life, and she would be perfectly happy after he had left. Of course she would.

Frances yawned luxuriously in the front seat. 'Well, I must say I won't be sorry to get down to London for the weekend. Do you want to drive, Hunter, or shall we go on the train?'

'The train's easier, I think.'

Well, so what if they were going to spend the weekend together? What had she expected? Gussie glowered out at the fields lying tranquil beneath the sun. If they wanted to waste their weekend in a dirty, crowded city, that was their problem! She couldn't care less!

She reminded herself how little she cared many times as Saturday dragged past at the wine bar, but, whenever she thought she had convinced herself, a vision of Hunter and Frances presented itself in vivid detail. She imagined them walking together, laughing together, making love together.

Gussie crashed the cutlery down on the table and began laying places with savage concentration.

'What's put you in such a filthy mood?' asked Tony, making a show of cowering away as he passed. 'Is anything the matter?'

'No,' said Gussie in a clipped voice. 'There is absolutely nothing the matter with me!'

But there was. She was jealous.

She stared unseeingly down at the knives and forks in her hand. Surely—*surely*—after all her warnings, she hadn't fallen in love with Hunter? The answer mocked her blindness. Of course she had.

Mindlessly, she continued setting the table. What a fool she had been! She could talk about Whin Farm till she was blue in the face, but it was Hunter who had been occupying her thoughts, Hunter whose kiss had lingered aggravatingly, tinging every meeting with that stomach-churning edge of excitement. It had been easy enough to tell herself that his was a merely physical attraction, easy to believe that she could never fall in love with a man who stood for everything she most despised. He was a developer; Whin Farm meant only money to him. He was a ruthless businessman who liked his women as smart and sophisticated as he was. He would be shaking the dust of Bracklewick off his shoes just as soon as he could. There was absolutely no future in loving him.

It didn't make it any easier not to, not when her heart clenched at the mere thought of him.

Gussie placed the glasses very carefully above each setting, wondering how she was going to get through the next few weeks. There was no point in hoping that Hunter would stay, or wishing that she was different. It had been stupid to let herself fall in love with him, and now she had she was just going to have to live with it.

She would get over it in the end, she told herself without too much hope. It would just be something else to chalk up to experience.

Her instinctive reaction was to run away and hide, just as she had fled to the woods when she was younger. She didn't think she could bear the torture of seeing him with Frances every day, but of course she would have to. Now that she had made her stand about Whin Farm, she couldn't back down. She would have to carry on as if her heart had never betrayed her, and rely on her pride to see her through without allowing Hunter to guess how she felt.

It shouldn't be too difficult to avoid being alone with him. Gussie's eyes stung as she contemplated the weeks ahead, wanting to be with Hunter, wanting to touch him, but condemned by her pride to keep her distance. Her heart cracked at the thought. It would be easier when he had gone altogether.

Behind her, Gussie heard the door tinkle to announce the arrival of more customers and she forced her mind back to the present. Her world might have fallen apart with the appalling realisation that she was in love with Hunter Scott, but Tony was still expecting her to help him cope with the Saturday rush.

The wine bar was crowded with weekend revellers and the chink of glass and crockery was almost lost in the confused babble of voices and laughter. There were several customers waiting for a table, so she had better pull herself together and get on with the job. She was at the bar, having just caught Tony's eye to let him know that the table was free when she saw who had come in, and she broke off in mid-sentence.

Hunter was standing just inside the door. He wore a suit and tie and was looking around as if searching for someone. Gussie couldn't take her eyes off him. There was an indefinable presence about him that made every other man in the room look a little dim, and drew almost every woman's eye. She could see them eyeing his dark, distinctive features and powerful physique appreciatively.

She was unprepared for the sight of him and her heart was jumping around so wildly that she clutched the empty tray to her chest as if to keep it in. It wasn't fair the way he could make her bones go weak just by standing there and *looking* like that.

Hunter's gaze swept over the room until his eyes finally found Gussie, still standing paralysed with surprise at the bar. He smiled and headed straight for her.

Gussie panicked. She couldn't face him, not yet. She needed time to hide the raw knowledge of her love before he read it in her eyes.

'I'll just take these to table five,' she muttered to Tony, grabbing some menus off the bar and turning her back deliberately on Hunter.

'But Gussie——' Tony began to point out that Hunter was coming to talk to her, but Gussie had gone.

Hunter was unfazed by her snub. He sat down calmly at the bar with the air of a man who was prepared to wait and chatted amicably with Tony, who was effusively friendly as if to make up for Gussie's rudeness.

Gussie lingered among the crowded tables as long as she could, watching them resentfully out of the corner of her eye. Her nerves were fluttering and her emotions whirled, joy at seeing him here on his own mingling with shock and desire and that overwhelming sense of panic in case he guessed how she felt. She *must* get herself under control!

Seizing an empty vegetable dish as an excuse, she went and skulked in the kitchen, where she pretended to wait for an order until the chef told her crisply to get out from under his feet. She sidled back into the restaurant and fiddled with the cutlery trays on the station, but a persistent customer eventually caught her eye for another bottle of wine and she was forced back to the bar.

Hunter was still there, talking to Tony. She stood as far away from him as possible, but the bar was crowded and Tony had sat him down at the very place usually reserved for her and Jane to shout their orders to him. It was impossible to ignore him.

'Hello, Gussie,' Hunter said, and only the slightest gleam at the back of his eyes showed that he had noticed her concerted efforts to avoid him.

'Hello,' she said curtly. She could feel his speculative gaze on her face, but kept her own eyes firmly fixed on Tony. 'Another bottle of Beaujolais for table eleven, please.'

'You seem busy tonight.'

'Yes.' Why were they having this stilted conversation when all she wanted to do was reach over and run her fingers over the strong brown hand that was curled around his glass, or touch her lips to the pulse beating in his throat? She wished Tony would hurry up with the wine. 'I thought you were in London,' she said ungraciously as the silence stretched uncomfortably.

Hunter shrugged. 'I decided I had too much to do up here. I've been working all day.' He was watching her averted profile with unnerving steadiness. 'I thought I'd give myself a day off tomorrow, though. It's going to be a nice day.' He paused. 'In fact, I just came in to ask if you were doing anything.'

'Tomorrow?' said Gussie, playing for time.

'Yes. I'd like to explore a bit more of the countryside round here and I wondered if you'd like to come with me. Walking, of course. I wouldn't dream of asking you to tear around in a car polluting the air unnecessarily!'

The teasing note in his voice unsettled Gussie and she shot him a suspicious look.

'Why me?' she asked baldly.

A half-smile touched the corners of his mouth. 'You know the countryside; I thought you'd make a good guide. And I don't know anyone else,' he added with disarming candour.

It wasn't quite what she wanted to hear, but Gussie felt a treacherous tug of temptation.

'We could take a picnic and make a day of it,' Hunter went on persuasively, and she risked another glance at him before jerking her eyes quickly back at Tony. Looking at him was dangerous.

Keep your distance, she reminded herself frantically. Pretend you don't want any more to do with him than you have to. It would be foolhardy to let herself get any more involved.

'I can't,' she muttered, shoring up her defences against temptation. 'I have to work tomorrow lunchtime.'

'I don't really need you till the evening,' Tony said quickly. He had been shamelessly eavesdropping as he uncorked the Beaujolais, his sharp eyes flickering between Gussie and Hunter. 'Jane can manage at

lunchtime. You take some time off and enjoy yourself
for a change, Gussie. You deserve it.'

'Well?' Hunter asked Gussie and, unfairly, he smiled,
crumbling all her best intentions at a stroke.

Tony's interference had left her with no excuse to cling
to, and the thought of spending a whole day alone with
Hunter tugged irresistibly at her mind. Surely one day
couldn't make much difference? She could pretend she
wasn't in love with him, could treat it as just an opportunity to persuade him about some of her ideas for
Whin Farm. Really, it would be like a job, she reasoned,
and anyway, she didn't have a choice now that Tony had
put his oar in. What harm could there be?

'All right,' she said, succumbing to temptation and
closing her mind to the inner voice which whispered that
her heart was still too vulnerable and that she would
regret it. 'I'll provide a picnic, shall I?' she offered, trying
to sound brisk but horribly aware of the quiver of excitement in her voice. They were only going for a *walk*,
for heaven's sake! It wasn't as if he'd invited her to a
romantic tryst by moonlight, she told herself sternly, but
it was impossible to stop her heart thumping in
anticipation.

'And I'll provide the wine,' Tony said, putting a bottle
of his best vintage on the counter before them. 'On the
house,' he added grandly.

Hunter held up his hands in mock-surrender. 'That
doesn't leave anything for me to take,' he protested, half
laughing.

'You can take Gussie,' said Tony, and Hunter turned
to watch the blush creeping up the pure line of her throat.

'The pleasure will be all mine,' he said.

CHAPTER SEVEN

WHEN Gussie woke the next morning, she was disgusted at her own lack of resolution. Hadn't she decided that it would be easier on herself to stay as far away from Hunter as possible? What on earth had possessed her to agree to spend a whole day with him? It was madness! She was supposed to be hardening her heart, not falling over herself at the slightest excuse to be with him.

But outside the sun was shining and the day beckoned, shimmering with promise. The lawn still glimmered with dew as Gussie leant out of the window and watched a blackbird tug determinedly at a worm in the flowerbed below. The worm had about as much chance of resisting as she did of denying her love for Hunter, she thought, and on an impulse she grabbed the first thing that came to hand, which happened to be her hairbrush, and threw it down at the blackbird. Startled, it dropped the worm and flew indignantly away.

If only it were that easy to get rid of her feelings for Hunter! Gussie turned back to her room and squared her shoulders. She would just have to be on her guard, that was all.

She was so offhand about Hunter as she made the sandwiches that her mother looked at her suspiciously, but Gussie refused to meet her eye. They were going for a walk and then she would come home. Surely she ought to be able to manage that without throwing herself into

Hunter's arms and begging him to make love to her. Gussie flinched as she imagined his reaction. No, she couldn't bear the humiliation of seeing the contemptuous mockery in his eyes, of being pushed hastily away and being told that she really wasn't his type.

By the time Hunter arrived, she was taut with nerves and was pacing restlessly around the house, wondering if she could persuade her mother to tell him that she had a headache and had changed her mind about going. When the knock at the door came, she jumped as if someone had let off a gun and looked wildly around for her mother, but she had mysteriously disappeared.

Her palms were damp and she wiped them on her jeans as she stood behind the door and took a few deep breaths in a desperate attempt to compose herself. Her legs were trembling, but she couldn't put it off any longer. Seizing the door, she jerked it open before she had time to lose her nerve again.

Hunter was standing a little back from the door, squinting up at the house, obviously wondering if there was anyone in. He wore blue jeans and a white polo shirt; the casual clothes made him look much younger, but did nothing to disguise the steely power of his body. He looked so solid, so distinct that Gussie's heart lurched uncontrollably, and when his gaze dropped to meet hers the impact of his personality was so strong that she felt as if she had been hit by a steam train.

She had never seen his eyes look so blue. His dark hair was slightly ruffled by the breeze, and Gussie had to grip the door-handle to stop herself reaching out for him.

He smiled at her, but she was so petrified of giving herself away that instead of smiling back as she wanted to do she scowled.

'Come in,' she said tightly.

If Hunter was perturbed by the lack of welcome, he gave no sign of it. He stepped past her into the cool hall, and Gussie flinched away from his nearness, terrified that he would brush against her as he passed and feel her burning with desire. She bent hastily to quieten the dogs, glad of the excuse to hide her face while she searched for something to say.

'Do you mind if we take the dogs with us?' It was the first thing that came into her head, and she could hear her voice was high and brittle.

'Of course not.' Hunter looked down at the two eccentrically shaped mongrels sniffing at his shoes and his mouth twitched. 'They can act as chaperons.'

Had he seen how nervous she was? Gussie straightened and shook back her hair, taking refuge behind a prickly barrier of pride. 'I'm sure that won't be necessary,' she said. 'They just want a walk.'

'Just like us?'

She didn't dare look at him. There was a dangerous undercurrent of laughter in his voice. He knew, she thought despairingly. He knew exactly why she was so edgy and was amused that anyone could get herself in such a state about going for a walk. It wasn't as if he hadn't made himself perfectly clear, she reminded herself as she stalked off to the kitchen in search of the sandwiches. He had asked her to be a guide for him because she knew the countryside and he didn't know anyone better, that was all. If a guide was what he wanted, a guide she would be.

She set off at a brisk pace, but if she'd hoped to make him struggle to keep up she was doomed to disappointment. He walked beside her with loose-jointed ease, and not even the steep climb up to the moors was enough to break his step. It was Gussie who was forced to stop first. She paused halfway up the hill and looked down at the valley basking in the sun below them while she caught her breath. The fields were lush and green between ancient hedgerows, and the sheep clustered in the shade of the trees. A tiny tractor trundled methodically up and down a slope at the far side of the valley and it was so quiet that they could just hear its mutter in the distance.

'What a peaceful view,' said Hunter. He didn't sound in the slightest bit out of breath, Gussie noted sourly.

'Yes,' she said, determined not to respond to his friendly overtures. Guides guided; they weren't supposed to make conversation as well.

Angus, the younger of the dogs, came bounding back to see what had happened to them, tongue lolling and plumed tail waving with impatience. To Gussie's chagrin, he made straight for Hunter. Normally, his devotion was reserved entirely for her, but he had taken to Hunter on sight and now he was busy sucking up to him.

'Come here, Angus,' she ordered and his ears flattened placatingly at the unaccustomed sharp note in her voice. Poor thing, she thought, patting him as he came obediently to her side. He's not to know that I'm jealous because I can't let Hunter know I love him like that. It was so much easier to be a dog and not have to pretend.

'I'm sorry. I'm trying to teach him not to jump up,' she said stiffly to Hunter, to excuse her sharpness.

'I don't mind. I like dogs, though I don't think I've ever seen one who looks as strange as he does,' he teased, eyeing Angus's comical proportions. 'I dread to think what's gone into his pedigree! Where on earth did you get him from?'

'I found him,' said Gussie. 'He'd been thrown out of a car on a back road.' Her eyes kindled with remembered indignation, and for a moment she forgot her awkwardness with Hunter. 'All his ribs were sticking out, and he'd been kicked and beaten, but he could still wag his tail at a kind word.'

Hunter glanced at the healthy, happy dog at her feet, and then at Gussie, who was looking fierce and protective, her amber eyes afire at the thought of such cruelty. His smile was slightly twisted.

'What about the other dog?'

'Ruby?' Gussie's eyes rested affectionately on the dog waiting patiently for them to move on. 'Ruby's only ever suffered from an excess of kindness. She belonged to an old lady who spoiled her rotten—you should have seen how fat she was! When the old lady died the vet was going to have to put Ruby down because they couldn't find a home for her, so I said I'd take her.'

'Lucky Ruby,' said Hunter, hunkering down to caress the dog's soft ears. He glanced up at Gussie again, his eyes blue and crinkled against the sun. 'You seem to have an endless fund of love for animals, Gussie. I hope there's some left to spare for mere humans?'

If only he knew how much! Gussie's eyes slid away from his. 'Only for some,' she said flatly.

'And what does one have to do to qualify for as much love as a dog or a badger or a rare orchid?' There was a strange note in his voice. 'Give away one's car? Abandon Whin Farm to the wild?'

'That would be a start,' said Gussie, hating the way he was playing with her. It was just a game to him. He didn't know that all he had had to do was walk into her life; *she* hadn't known until she met him how strong and how deep and how hopeless it was possible for love to be. 'Shall we go?' she suggested coldly, before he could say any more.

They stopped for lunch high on the moors, perching on a rocky outcrop above the heather. Hunter produced Tony's bottle from his haversack, and they sipped at the wine in silence.

Gussie leant back against the warm rock and let the breeze lift her hair away from her hot face as her edginess faded in the wild beauty of the scene. Everything was sharply in focus; she could see each spike of heather with its tiny leaves and twisted woody stems. The dogs snuffled happily along the narrow sheep tracks and a solitary hawk hovered on the bright air.

Hunter was sitting beside her, not too close. His legs were bent and his arms rested on his knees, his hands loosely clasped between them. His profile was etched against the deep blue of the sky, and Gussie was unable to prevent a shiver of happiness just to know that he was there.

He couldn't possibly have seen her spine shudder, but he glanced at her as if he had sensed her awareness. Her cheeks were flushed with exertion still, and her eyes were full of sunshine.

'I'm glad you came with me,' he said. 'I would never have found this place by myself.'

Gussie's happiness dimmed at the reminder of her role as guide. She sat forward and wrapped her arms around her knees as if for comfort. 'You'll be able to come on your own next time,' she said with a brittle smile.

'I don't know that there'll be time to come again,' he said, regretfully. 'There's a lot to do in the next few weeks. You're lucky, you can come here any time, but the rest of us have to go back to London.'

At any other time, Gussie would have agreed about how lucky she was to live here, but now, she realised dismally, the moors would just be another place where Hunter wasn't. When he left he would take her pleasure in the countryside with him.

'Yes, I'm lucky,' she agreed quietly.

'Would you ever consider leaving here, Gussie, or will you be happy to spend your whole life with your woods and moors?'

She could almost have believed that her answer mattered to him, but when she risked a curious glance he was patting Angus, who had flopped down beside him. Gussie's toes curled inside her shoes at the sight of his strong hand smoothing over the dog's coat. Angus sighed and stretched with pleasure as she watched enviously. She would have done the same, she thought, imagining how it would feel if Hunter's hand were smoothing over her skin instead. Her nerves tingled at the very thought, and she averted her eyes quickly.

'As long as I know the woods and the moors will always be here to come back to, I don't mind where I go.'

'But you wouldn't be happy living in a city?' he asked with strange persistence.

Would she be happy living in London with him? 'No,' she said at last. 'No, I don't think I would. I'd like to see places wilder than here.' She gave a half-embarrassed shrug. 'I suppose I've always imagined myself going off to save the rainforest somewhere when I left, but there's no point in going until I've got some useful experience to offer. That's why I joined Future Green.'

'Future Green will only give you experience in how to make a nuisance of yourself,' Hunter said caustically, and her chin went up.

'Maybe, but sometimes that's what's required.'

'You're not regretting your break with them, are you?'

Gussie sighed. She missed the certainties of Future Green. The group's activities had taken up so much of her time that she didn't know what she was going to do with herself when Hunter had no more need of her. She would just have to do something positive about getting that job she had always talked about.

'No,' she said, leaning back on her hands. 'As long as I feel I'm doing something useful for you.'

Hunter put his hand over hers before she had time to realise what he was doing and snatch it away. 'You *are* doing something useful,' he said. 'I'll listen to any suggestions you have to make about Whin Farm, Gussie, I promise. Working for me will be far better experience than waving banners with Future Green.'

His hand seemed to burn through hers on to the rock. Gussie was sure that she could feel every line on his palm, every whorl on his fingertips. Taken by surprise, her first instinct was to turn her hand beneath his so that their palms met and their fingers entwined, but she stopped herself just in time.

'I know,' she muttered, wishing he would never take his hand away, wishing that he would never let her go.

Hunter lifted his hand. 'Shall we have those sandwiches now?'

Gussie jumped up as if she'd been scalded. 'I'll get them.'

'I've been wondering what you've put in them all the way up here,' he told her, watching her unwrap the sandwiches. 'I thought ham would be nice, but then I decided it was more likely to be seaweed or raw carrot or tofu and beansprouts.'

'Cheese and gooseberry chutney,' she corrected him, trying, but failing, to look offended. It was easier to deal with teasing than with his hand over hers and that warm, serious look in his eyes. Keep it light-hearted, she told herself. 'I hope that's all right?'

'It's all right for *me*,' he said, pretending to sound shocked. 'But what about the gooseberries? I don't know how you could spread your chutney with an easy conscience, Gussie! How would you like to be torn off the bush and made into chutney without so much as a by-your-leave?'

Gussie made as if to throw a sandwich at him before she gave in and laughed. A gust of wind blew her glinting hair about as she scrambled back on to the rocks and handed him the packet.

'You remind me of my brothers,' she said.

'Do I?' Hunter sounded startled. 'I hope you don't think of me as a brother?'

She kept her head bent over her sandwich. 'They think I'm ridiculous too,' she said, not answering his question. 'Why is it that people find it laughable when you believe in something?'

'Perhaps we feel a little ashamed that our own beliefs don't stand up to comparison,' said Hunter. 'We laugh to make ourselves feel better about our own inadequacies.'

'I can't believe you feel inadequate about anything!' Gussie said involuntarily, and he half smiled.

'Can't you? I certainly don't have your passionate belief in a green world.'

'Well, no, but you must feel passionately about something!'

Hunter turned his head to look at her. She was sitting cross-legged on the rock feeding her crusts to the two dogs who slavered beseechingly and followed every movement of hand to mouth with rigid concentration. Her face was almost hidden by the coppery cloud of hair and her lashes swept down to guard her wide, wary eyes.

'I do,' he said. 'But I have to feel that my passion can be reciprocated. Caring for the environment is a worthy cause, Gussie, but don't you ever wish it felt as passionately about you as you do about it? As I told you before, I think there are more important things to feel passionately about. Don't you remember?'

Gussie froze. Of course she remembered. She remembered the feel of his mouth against hers, the touch of his hands. She remembered the deep, quivering excitement and the way her skin had shivered beneath his fingers.

She didn't want to look at him, but her eyes felt as if they were being dragged towards his, and when they met she suddenly found it difficult to breathe. She couldn't read his expression, but something about it made her heart turn over.

'You remember, don't you, Gussie?'

'Yes, I remember,' she whispered.

Very slowly, Hunter reached out and brushed the soft hair away from her face, letting his fingers linger against her cheek. Gussie's heart slowed until she thought it would stop. The world had shrunk until it encompassed no more than the feel of his skin against hers.

'I can't help feeling your passion's rather wasted on the environment,' he said thoughtfully and his touch tightened.

Gussie began to tremble. He's going to kiss me, she thought, knowing that she should pull away before she was utterly lost but unable to tear her eyes away from his.

She was saved by the RAF. A low-flying jet on manoeuvres streaked overhead, followed seconds later by a great whoosh of sound. It seemed to come out of nowhere and they jerked apart in shock as the noise smashed the vibrating tension between them as if they had been enclosed in a bubble of glass.

Gussie took a gulp of air and shook her head slightly to clear it. Raw disappointment warred with relief as she realised how close she had been to dissolving in his arms. Risking a glance at Hunter, she saw that he was looking so normal that for a moment she wondered if she had imagined the whole incident. But her cheek was still tingling where he had touched her, and her pulse drummed in her ears.

'You don't want to become obsessive,' he said, exactly as if nothing had happened.

Nothing *had* happened, she reminded herself. He had touched her cheek, that was all. Bitter resentment that he could be so careless of her feelings sharpened her tongue.

'I can do without your advice!'

He shrugged. 'I know to my cost what happens to women when they become obsessed with one idea.'

'What do you mean?'

She thought he might not tell her, but after a pause he said, 'I lived for two years with a woman called Imogen. Your father met her. She was beautiful, smart, intelligent, and it took me all that time to realise that when it came down to it she would always put her career before me. She wasn't really interested in anything else.' He couldn't quite hide the bitterness in his voice. 'It was a relief to both of us when I left and we agreed to go our separate ways. I never want to get involved with anyone like Imogen again. I want to be the first interest in a woman's life, not the second.'

'How very self-centred of you,' Gussie said crisply, retreating behind her prickles. She was horribly afraid that Hunter had been warning her off. She might not be beautiful, smart or intelligent, but in Hunter's book she was just like Imogen. Gussie had never considered her concern for the environment in the light of an obsession before. Yes, she loved the country and cared deeply about what happened to it, but Hunter inspired a quite different sort of passion in her.

Hunter shot her a sharp look, and she prayed that he couldn't read her expression as accurately as he sometimes seemed to be able to do. This was just the kind of situation she had dreaded. Any minute now, Hunter would point an accusing finger at her and tell her that she was jealous, jealous of an unknown woman called Imogen who had thrown away the love that Gussie longed for. There was no point in her wishing she didn't feel so strongly about the environment, he would say, because he would never love her anyway.

But all he said was, 'Perhaps. But if I ever found a girl like that, she would be at the centre of my life, too. I've had enough of half-hearted relationships. It's all or nothing as far as I'm concerned.'

'Now who sounds obsessive?' Gussie snapped, bitterly aware of how hopeless it was to long for Hunter to make *her* the centre of his life.

The atmosphere was strained as they walked down the hill. Gussie tried to console herself with the knowledge that she hadn't given herself away, but it was cold comfort. He couldn't have made it plainer that she had no future with him, but it was impossible not to wonder what would have happened if they hadn't been sitting under an RAF flight path. She had been so sure that he was going to kiss her.

Gussie stumped down the hill and told herself that she was glad he hadn't. She ought to write to the RAF and withdraw the letter she had sent last year demanding that they stop low-level flying!

Hunter strode silently beside her, his mouth set in a strangely grim line. Once, when Gussie tripped in the heather, his hand shot out to steady her, but when she flinched at the jarring electricity of his touch his brows snapped together and he dropped her arm abruptly.

That night, Gussie gave herself a good talking-to. From now on, she really *would* avoid him as much as possible. She owed her pride that much. She would go into the office as she had promised, of course, but she would be brisk and businesslike and neither Hunter nor Frances would guess that her heart was breaking.

To her relief, Hunter was out at a meeting with the local planning officials for most of the first morning. Frances ignored Gussie, sitting in the corner and studying the plans Hunter had given her before he left. Gussie didn't mind, but it was more difficult to ignore them in her turn the next day when Hunter was back. He and Frances obviously got on well together and they dealt with the problems that arose with the same ruthless efficiency.

Gussie couldn't decide how Hunter felt about Frances, but it didn't take much to guess how Frances felt about him. She was playing things very carefully, though, Gussie realised bleakly, recognising that Frances was amusing and clever and far too sophisticated to get obsessive about anything. Gussie was certain that she had heard about Imogen's preoccupation with her career, and was making sure that Hunter knew that she was a quite different type of woman, no matter how indispensable she might be in the office.

In her corner, Gussie kept her head bent over the plans and tried not to notice how Hunter smiled at Frances or drank his coffee or rubbed his jaw when he was thinking. His dark presence in the office was impossible to ignore, but whenever she found her eyes straying towards him she would wrench them firmly back to her desk. She was here for Whin Farm, and she didn't want to give him any reason to forget it.

On the third morning, she presented Hunter with her preliminary list of suggestions. She had on her most prickly air, and sat stiffly on the chair in front of his desk while he studied her list. His dark brows drew together in concentration, and she was ready to look aloof and unconcerned when he put the paper down and fixed her with that disconcertingly keen stare of his. There was more grey than blue in his eyes today, and it gave him a colder, more ruthless look that went with his dark suit. Gussie could hardly recognise the casual, carefree man who had stood on her doorstep on Sunday with the blue sky reflected in his eyes.

'Do you realise how much it would cost if I implemented all your suggestions?' he asked at last.

'Principles don't come cheaply,' said Gussie. 'You said it was in your interests to make the leisure complex as environmentally friendly as possible. I'm just telling you how you can do that.'

Hunter eyed her narrowly before he dropped his gaze to the list once more. 'I take your point about solar power, but we couldn't rely on it. A complex this size needs an alternative source of power, but we could use solar panels to heat, say, the swimming-pool and saunas.' He tapped his finger against the paper as he skimmed down the list. 'I can see the point in having energy-saving light bulbs as well, and I certainly wasn't contemplating having doors made out of tropical hardwoods, so that's not a problem. But do we really need to worry about whether the wood preservatives in the roof are poisonous to bats? Nobody's going to know the difference.'

'A bat would,' said Gussie.

'Possibly, but I'm afraid bats aren't my priority.'

'If you want to sell yourself as a company that really cares about the environment, you're going to have to change your priorities,' she said stubbornly. 'You can ease your conscience by making a few high-profile decisions which everyone will notice and applaud, but often it's the things you don't do that matter as much as those you do.'

She gestured at the pile of Press releases on his desk with their stunning pictures of the meadow at Whin Farm. Frances had written a very effective piece describing how Scott Developments were at the forefront of environmental awareness and how they were going to preserve this rare site. 'It's easy to feel good about preserving something pretty like a meadow, but I think you could present yourself as a company that really *does* care, not just another London organisation dressing up the facts with a lot of misleading froth. Bats and wood preservatives may not make such good material for your precious Press releases, but if you're going to dismiss them just because "nobody's going to know the difference", then you've got no right to claim that you're any more concerned about the environment than anyone else.'

'All right,' said Hunter, holding up his hand as she paused for breath. 'Calm down! I take your point, but I'm proposing that we operate as an example of environmental awareness, not a shrine. We can't do everything, and I won't be suggesting that we have. However, I *will* reconsider how the roof timbers are treated, if that makes you feel any better.'

Gussie didn't like the amusement that lurked at the back of his eyes, but she nodded.

Hunter returned to the list. 'I'm happy to put badger gates in the fences, and I think the idea of building proper hides in the woods is a good one, but I have to confess that I don't see the relevance of making sure that the chefs take the lids off any tins they open.' He raised an enquiring eyebrow and Gussie flushed.

'If you don't take the lid off completely, and the cans get thrown out, the little field animals like mice and shrews get trapped inside them. You see, the lid gets pushed in, and they think it looks like a cosy shelter, so they push in, but then they haven't got the strength to push the lid out again and they just starve.' She stopped, realising that Hunter was looking unconvinced.

'I think on that point you'll have to try and convert the chefs themselves at a later date,' he said sardonically. 'I sincerely hope they won't be using many tins anyway, and if they do that they'll be disposed of properly instead of being chucked out into the field to trap unwary field mice!'

'You could have special dustbins for recycling cans,' she suggested eagerly and he sighed.

'I wondered when recycling was going to come up!' He ran his pen down her list again, ticking a number of points, before he handed it back to her. 'I'd like you to look into those suggestions I've marked. These are just ideas at the moment. Now I want to know exactly how effective they are in practice, how much they would cost, where we can get them from, what maintenance is required, that sort of thing. When you've got all those details, come back to me and I'll look at your proposals again.'

Gussie was surprised at how much she enjoyed doing the research for Hunter. It was the first time she had studied the details rather than the ideas, and although she regretfully decided that one or two of her suggestions just weren't going to be practicable she was sure that Hunter would agree that the others were well worth the money involved.

Every morning, she spent a couple of hours at the office before going off to the wine bar. She was still guarded, and hid her feelings for Hunter behind a cloak of prickly aloofness, but it helped to throw herself into the task he had given her. It made it easier to pretend that Whin Farm was still her only interest.

Hunter was equally brusque and remote, but sometimes she caught him watching her with a speculative look. If their eyes ever met, the air between them would jangle with unacknowledged tension, and they would both look quickly away.

Frances was busy organising a slick publicity campaign, and she was put out to find that the best reaction of all came from an interview Gussie was persuaded to give on local radio. Word had got round of her change of allegiance, and she had to face some tough questions about how she could justify working for a property developer given her views on the environment, but the reporter didn't ask her any questions that Gussie hadn't already asked herself. She gave such an impassioned defence of the Whin Farm project that they had a stream of visitors to see the designs for themselves and offer their support.

Hunter came into the office the next day holding a copy of the local paper. Frances was out, following up on Gussie's success with rather bad grace, and Gussie was alone. She was standing by the photocopier, reading an article about how shire horses could be used to clear woodlands instead of tractors and wondering if she could persuade Hunter to consider it. She put the magazine down uncertainly when Hunter arrived.

As always when they were alone, the atmosphere tightened imperceptibly, and Gussie moistened her lips.

'Nothing's wrong, is it?'

'Quite the opposite.' Hunter opened the paper and showed her a full-page spread based on her interview, including a picture of Gussie looking vehement and an artist's impression of the new complex. '"Local campaigner speaks out in favour of new development,"' he read the headline, and skimmed on down through the article to quote the best bits. '"Augusta Blake's moving defence of her beliefs... few can doubt that she would commit herself to any project that would harm this area... Hunter Scott's most valuable asset may well be her support..."' He handed her the paper so that she could see for herself and grinned suddenly. 'How does it feel to be my most valuable asset?'

'Unlikely,' said Gussie, letting her hair tumble forward to hide her face as she pretended to read the article, but Hunter took her chin in his hand and forced her to look at him.

'It's not at all unlikely. I have to confess that I wasn't sure whether you would be more trouble than you were worth when I first offered you this job, but you've proved yourself to be a real asset. That one interview has done more to sway local opinion in favour of the project than anything else. It can't have been easy to admit that you left Future Green to come and work for me, and I'm grateful. In fact, I'm not just grateful,' he added seriously, 'I'm proud of you.'

He looked down into her eyes, which had deepened to a dark gold as hopeless desire ensnared her, and then his gaze dropped to her mouth. Gussie felt him hesitate, and a thrill of anticipation ran through her, but when he bent his head he moved his head at the last moment, and kissed her on the cheek instead.

CHAPTER EIGHT

IT WAS the briefest of contacts but Gussie's heart jolted, and Hunter stepped back quickly as if he too had felt the scorch of awareness.

He cleared his throat. 'The director of the company which is going to manage Whin Farm is coming up tomorrow,' he said, moving away a little too casually. 'I'd like you to come up with me and help show him round the site. And see if Tony will let you have tomorrow evening off. We'll be taking Jim out to dinner, and it would be nice if you could come too.'

Jim Barker turned out to be a round, friendly man with shrewd brown eyes. He took to Gussie at once, and she was delighted that Whin Farm would end up in such capable hands, even if his presence was an all too bitter reminder that Hunter would be returning to London as soon as the building got under way. That knowledge twisted like a knife in her heart and she had to bite her lip to keep herself from gasping. There was no point in thinking about that now. She should be thinking instead about the future of Whin Farm. Jim was impressed by her knowledge of the countryside, and took many of her ideas much more seriously than she had dared hope. That ought to be enough.

Tony had been happy to let Gussie swap her night off with Jane, and she waited apprehensively for Hunter the next evening. Frances and Jim had a meeting together that afternoon, and would go to the restaurant together, so Hunter had announced brusquely that he would pick her up. When she had protested, he had frowned.

'Don't be ridiculous!' he snapped. 'You can't turn up at Bellingham Hall on your bike!'

As soon as she had learnt that the dinner would be at the most expensive restaurant in the district, Gussie had gone out and splurged her meagre savings on a new dress. She would look pretty and feminine for once, she vowed, and perhaps—perhaps—Hunter would look at her with new eyes. In the car, she smoothed the skirt nervously over her knees, but as soon as she saw Frances waiting with Jim in the library bar she knew that she might as well have saved her money and worn her old grey dress instead. The green and white print which had seemed so pretty in the shop looked cheap and fussy next to Frances's stunningly simple black dress.

Gussie wriggled uncomfortably in her chair. How could she ever have hoped to impress Hunter? She felt awkward and ugly and out of place, and the hushed elegance of the dining-room did nothing to put her at her ease.

She scowled down at the menu, wishing that she hadn't agreed to come. There were no vegetarian dishes on the menu either.

'I think I'll have the duck,' Frances decided, smiling charmingly at the two men.

Gussie dropped her menu. 'Duck?' she echoed, her voice rising in horror. 'You can't have duck!'

'Why on earth not?' Frances asked irritably.

'Ducks mate for life!'

'Oh, for heaven's sake!' Frances sighed. 'Just because you're a vegetarian, it doesn't mean everybody else has to be. I find duck absolutely delicious.'

Gussie's blood boiled at her indifference. 'How can you possibly enjoy eating a creature, knowing that its mate will be left alone for the rest of its life?'

'That's just sentimental nonsense,' snapped Frances. Noticing the interested stares of the other diners who were patently eavesdropping on the gathering scene, she pinned her bright smile back on her face and hissed at Gussie between her teeth. 'And will you please keep your voice down? We don't want a scene.'

'Why not?' Gussie asked loudly. 'We ought to have more scenes about facts that make us uncomfortable, or make us realise just how cruel and inhumane we really are.' She looked defiantly around the room, golden eyes ablaze. 'I'd feel like a murderer if I ate duck,' she announced in the same carrying voice, and several people dropped their eyes guiltily to their plates.

Her chin was still tilted in challenge as her gaze came back to her companions. Frances was looking scandalised, Jim Barker amused, but Hunter had a strangely arrested expression in his eyes as he watched her vivid face, and as Gussie's gaze met his her indignation faded away to be replaced by something deeper and far more disturbing, and she felt herself begin to tremble inside.

Dropping her eyes, she crumbled a bread roll between her fingers, hardly aware of what she was doing. She had seen amusement in his eyes, and a sort of exasperated admiration, but there had been something else as well, something that made her heart thump insistently and her pulse boom in her ears.

Frances was complaining in a furious whisper about Gussie's eccentricities, but Gussie didn't hear a word. She was staring down at her roll, wondering where she would ever find the strength to resist if Hunter looked like that again, and where she would find the strength to survive after he had left if she didn't.

'I think we should order.' Hunter's voice cut through her jumbled thoughts. 'Gussie?'

She jerked her head up, remembering just in time not to look at him. 'Oh...' She ran her eye blindly down the menu again, but her first impression had been right: it was a carnivore's dream. 'I'll just have a selection of vegetables if that's all right.'

'I'm sure we can find you something more exciting than that,' Jim Barker protested, and Hunter caught the waiter's eye.

'Yes, we can,' he said grimly, and asked to see the manager, who was duly impressed by the card he proffered.

Without once raising his voice, Hunter managed to reduce the suave manager to ingratiating stutters. Why were there no vegetarian dishes on the menu? he demanded. Did the manager not believe in catering for the tastes of a discerning minority and was he not aware of the moral issues involved in featuring duck on his menus?

The manager was clearly not aware of anything of the kind, but he knew perfectly well who Hunter was and he was anxious not to antagonise such an influential customer, so he nodded and agreed that the matter should be seriously considered.

'In the meantime,' Hunter went on smoothly, 'I would appreciate it if your chef would make an effort to produce something special for my colleague, Miss Blake.'

'Certainly, certainly.' The manager bowed himself off, leaving Gussie unsure of whether she wanted to laugh or cry. Frances knew no such uncertainty; she was furious.

'I don't know what you're playing at,' she whispered fiercely to Hunter. 'This is a respectable restaurant. We'll never be able to show our faces in here again after the scene you just made! He thought you were quite mad! Gussie must be used to people thinking her eccentric, but I'd have thought you'd have had more sense.'

She turned pointedly back to Jim before she could notice Hunter catch Gussie's eye, or the fleeting instinctive smile of complicity they shared. She was even more put out when Gussie got the best meal of the lot, a selection of delicate vegetable *timbales* with a light, herby sauce. The duck, which she had insisted on having, was tough.

The chef would have been distraught to know how little Gussie noticed of the dish he had prepared with such care. She ate it all, and asked the waiter to pass on her thanks for all his effort, but the truth was that she hardly tasted it. Hunter's brief smile burned inside her eyelids. He talked to Jim and Frances, but his gaze kept entangling with hers in a wordless exchange that set her heart thudding and her senses tingling.

Gussie knew that she should make an effort to join in the conversation, but her tongue felt thick and unwieldy, and the sound of her pulse roaring in her ears made it impossible to concentrate on anything other than the cool, exciting line of his mouth and the disturbing light in his eyes that held her in thrall.

A frantic inner voice warned her to be on her guard, to remember all that she had told herself about not getting involved, but it was shouted down by her senses clamouring to touch him again. Gussie had to grip her wine glass, so strong was the urge to reach across the table and feel the warmth of his skin beneath her fingers. Thank goodness they were leaving.

With a tremendous effort, she forced herself to look at Jim. 'I think you've got something with this conservation business,' he was saying to Hunter as Gussie tuned in. 'Why don't you come down to London with me tomorrow, Hunter, and we'll see if we can persuade my board to take this approach in our other centres?'

Hunter hesitated, his eyes flickering to Gussie, but when he spoke she decided she must have imagined the reluctance in his expression. 'Good idea,' he said easily enough to Jim at last. 'We've got the go-ahead from the authorities up here, so Frances can hold the fort for a few days.'

He was leaving the next day. Gussie clung to the thought as if for protection as Hunter held the car door open for her. He was going to London, where he belonged; when he came back, it wouldn't be for long. She must ignore this quivering tension between them and remember how little place there would ever be for her in his life.

They drove in silence. As arranged, Frances had taken Jim back to his hotel, and Hunter had ignored Gussie's faint mutterings about a taxi. The blue-black of the sky was a-shimmer with stars, and the countryside lay still and quiet, bathed in the ghostly moonlight like a negative from a picture postcard. Gussie recited all the reasons why she should keep a firm control on her emotions, but she felt hollow with a deep, aching desire, and all she could think about was the tantalising nearness of his body, the excitement that shivered down her spine whenever she looked at his mouth.

When Hunter cut the engine outside the house, the silence between them tautened until Gussie was sure that it would snap at the least sound. She couldn't look at Hunter as she stared straight ahead, willing herself to move. All she had to do was say thank you and good-night, and get out of the car. She would be safe then. But the silence held her frozen, afraid to move in case she shattered the tension, and in the end Hunter came round to open the door for her.

Gussie climbed out, moving stiffly like a puppet, and heard the door click to behind her. Hunter was standing very close, making it impossible for her to step away from the car without brushing against him.

With an effort, she cleared her throat. 'Thank you,' she said, appalled at how husky her voice sounded.

'What for?' he asked softly. They were staring at each other as if transfixed, and the conversation they were having had nothing to do with what their eyes were saying.

'For... for...' Gussie was adrift. She couldn't remember what she was supposed to be talking about, why they were talking at all, and when Hunter cupped her face in his hands she could only trail into silence and stare helplessly up at him with eyes that gleamed dark and dazed in the moonlight. It was too late for words.

Hunter's hands slid back to tangle in her silky hair. For a long, long moment he looked down into her face, and then his hands tightened almost painfully as he bent his head and kissed her.

Any lingering thoughts of resistance vanished with the first touch of his mouth, and Gussie abandoned herself to the searing pleasure of deep, hungry kisses that sent her senses spinning. Hunter surfaced for a muttered exclamation before pressing her against the car, his body hard and insistent, but she was oblivious to the metal digging into her back while his lips plundered hers and his hands explored the smooth warmth of her skin.

Gussie was on fire. She gasped with excitement beneath his touch, sliding her arms around his back to pull him even closer. The desire that had simmered between them all evening had burst into flames with a speed which would have shocked her if she had been capable of thinking sensibly, and it burnt now at the very limits of control as she melted into his lean strength and gave back kiss for kiss. The fact that Hunter would never want to get involved, the knowledge that he would soon be leaving for good, no longer seemed important. For now, all that mattered was the warmth of his kisses and the thrill of his hard body beneath her hands.

She longed for him to lay her down and make love to her there and then in the cool moonlight, but reality filtered back as Hunter pulled away at last. He did so very gradually, letting his lips drift along Gussie's jaw and down her throat as if reluctant to let her go.

'I think *I* should be thanking *you*,' he said, lifting his head with a last lingering kiss at the corner of her mouth where it curved into a smile. 'I've been wanting to kiss you all evening.' He smoothed the soft, tousled hair away from her face. 'I'd really like to go on kissing you,' he admitted with a rueful smile, 'but I won't be able to answer for the consequences if I do, and I'm supposed to be leaving with Jim at the crack of dawn. I shouldn't be away too long, though, and when I get back I think you and I should have a talk, don't you?' When Gussie only nodded, still too dazed to think clearly, he dropped his arms, leaving her leaning weakly against the car. 'I hate to go like this,' he muttered savagely, watching her face.

'It's all right,' whispered Gussie, finding her voice with difficulty. 'I understand.'

Hunter looked down at her. 'Do you, Gussie?' he said. 'I wonder if you do?'

It wasn't until the next day that Gussie began to wonder what he meant.

She was still glowing when she woke up, still dazzled by the memory of Hunter's kisses. He hadn't said he loved her, he hadn't said he would stay, but he had wanted to go on kissing her, and he promised to come back soon. It was enough to send her heart soaring with hope.

Gussie felt translated, vibrant, *alive*. Her senses tingled with an uncanny awareness and the summer morning seemed to shimmer with joy as she cycled into Bracklewick. Hunter had kissed her as if he loved her. The hedgerows had never been so bright with flowers, the wind had never been so exhilarating against her face as she free-wheeled down the hills.

She was smiling as she pushed open the door into the office, but her smile faded when she saw that her desk had been cleared.

'Where are all my notes?' she asked Frances when the other woman appeared from the kitchen with a cup of coffee.

Frances strolled over to her desk and put the cup down with an insulting lack of concern. 'I really think this charade had gone on long enough, don't you?'

'What charade?' Gussie asked blankly.

'All this nonsense about you making suggestions for the Whin Farm project.' Frances sat down and began flicking over the pages of a report. 'You don't really think a professional firm like Scott Developments is going to take any notice of the local crank, do you?'

'But Hunter said——'

'Oh, Hunter's very indulgent, I know,' Frances interrupted her with some contempt. 'He's got a notoriously soft spot for a pretty girl, but you really mustn't confuse his attempts to be kind with his position as director of his firm. He's worked hard to set up Scott Developments, and its interests are paramount. I joined him right at the start, and I can tell you that he won't do anything that's likely to jeopardise the success of his company.'

'He said that environmental issues were important,' Gussie protested.

'They are,' Frances said coolly. 'They make a good selling point for the project, but that's precisely why he's not going to risk its success by relying on you. No one's denying that you're the ultimate country girl, but your approach is hardly professional. Hunter needs someone who'll give him the facts, not the sentiment.' She paused,

raising a perfectly pencilled eyebrow at Gussie's mutinous expression. 'Why do you think Hunter's gone to
London?'

'Because Jim asked him to attend a meeting,' Gussie
said bravely, but Frances's smile sent a shiver of fore-
boding down her spine.

'A meeting to appoint a *professional* environmental
consultant,' she said with relish. 'If you'd been listening
to the discussion last night instead of staring at Hunter
like some love-struck teenager, you'd have heard for
yourself. So you see, there isn't much point in you
hanging around any longer.'

When Gussie merely stared at her blindly, Frances went
on with an edge of impatience, 'It would be much less
embarrassing all round if you weren't here when Hunter
gets back. He really hasn't got time to deal with adolescent crushes at this stage of the project.'

An adolescent crush? Was that all it seemed to Hunter?
The glow of happiness drained slowly from Gussie's face.
What had Hunter said, after all? That they would talk.
Had he meant to take her aside and tell her kindly that
her feelings were embarrassingly obvious?

'I see,' she whispered. 'In that case I'd better go.'

Outside, the sunshine seemed to mock her. Gussie
stood in the middle of the pavement, trying to hang on
to the memory of the kisses she had shared with Hunter
last night, but Frances's words, clear and cutting, kept
beating in her brain. She wanted desperately to believe
that Frances was wrong, that their kisses had meant as
much to Hunter as they had to her, but the other woman
had been so sure of herself that Gussie's confidence
began to seep away. She might have convinced herself

that Frances was simply jealous, but there had been a triumphant ring of truth in her news about the professional consultant, too. If she was right about that, might she not be right about everything else?

Turning, she drifted aimlessly along the pavement. She felt miserably uncertain, afraid to remember too much in case her memories bore out what Frances had said—that Hunter had meant to get a professional consultant all the time. She wouldn't mind so much if only he had told her instead of pretending to take her seriously. The humiliating realisation that he might just have been amusing himself made Gussie clench her hands. She would rather believe that he had encouraged her to keep her quiet!

At least she hadn't told him that she loved him. Gussie was honest enough to know that if Hunter hadn't left when he did she would have blurted it out, and her battered pride clung to the thought that she had spared herself that humiliation. As it was, she didn't know whether to feel wretched or angry, nor whether it was with Frances or Hunter or herself. She had known the risks of falling in love with a man like Hunter, she reminded herself bitterly. She could give him the benefit of the doubt and lay herself open to more heartbreak, or she could gather the tattered rags of her pride about her and pretend that she didn't care, just as she should have done long ago.

Over the next few days, Gussie swung between the two. One minute she would be blazing with anger, and the next longing just to see Hunter and hear him explain that it was all a terrible mistake. Immersed in her own problems, she hardly noticed what was going on around her, until one day a voice calling her name broke through her preoccupation.

Gussie was locking up her bike outside the wine bar, and she straightened with some wariness when she recognised Julia, one of the Future Green protesters who had come on that first, ill-fated demonstration at Whin Farm. She shrugged dismissively when Gussie asked after the group.

'As a matter of fact, I've left Future Green too. We never seemed to achieve anything, and I got fed up with Simon and Mark carrying on like a couple of dictators.' She glanced curiously at Gussie. 'They were really put out by your going off to work for Hunter Scott. I've never seen them so vindictive. They went on and on about how you'd betrayed all your principles, but the more I thought about it, the more I realised that you'd actually chosen to do something constructive for a change.'

Had she done something constructive, or had she just let Hunter Scott make a fool out of her? Gussie's doubts came rushing back and she bent her head over her bike and fiddled with the lock, unwilling to meet Julia's eyes. 'I did what I thought was best for Whin Farm,' she said at last.

'You'll never convince Simon or Mark about *that*!' Julia looked glum. 'They won't rest until they've forced Scott Developments out of Whin Farm. It's become a matter of pride since you left, and especially since that radio interview you gave. They lost a lot of support after that, and they think that if they let you and Scott get away with it people will start to wonder what the point is of a group like Future Green.'

'They're not going to do anything stupid, are they?' Gussie asked, suddenly fearful, and Julia hesitated.

'I did overhear some talk about setting fire to the disused outbuildings at Whin Farm. Now that Jack Wilson has left, they said it wouldn't affect any animals, but it would cost Scott a lot to repair and would show that they really mean business.'

'They can't do that!' Horrified, Gussie stared at her, Hunter and her own emotions forgotten. 'There are swallows nesting in the barn!'

Julia shrugged. 'They might have decided not to do it,' she suggested, but Gussie wasn't prepared to take the risk.

'I'll have to talk to Simon,' she said. Even if it were not for the disastrous consequences to the wildlife if the fire burnt out of control, she couldn't stand aside and let Future Green ruin Hunter's plans.

Taking her courage in her hands, she rang Simon and asked to meet him. He obviously thought that she had changed her mind and wanted to come crawling back to Future Green, and leapt at the chance to crow. They arranged to meet at the health food shop the next morning. It had a few tables in the window where they served snacks and drinks, and Gussie was there early, nursing a pineapple juice and hoping desperately that Simon would turn up.

He did, but their meeting was not a success. When he found out that she was far from wanting to rejoin Future Green, Simon sneered, and refused to listen to her arguments. He was evasive when she questioned him about their plans for Whin Farm.

'You never did have any guts, Gus,' he jeered. 'Even if we *did* have a plan like that, do you think I'd tell a traitor like you?'

'Simon, *please*!' Gussie leant forward and put her hand on his arm imploringly. 'I don't care what happens to Hunter Scott,' she lied. 'I just want to make sure that none of the wildlife at Whin Farm will get hurt.'

But Simon shrugged every argument aside. She was as naïve and sentimental as ever, he told her. She simply didn't understand the need for direct action.

Gussie was reluctant to give up, but when it was clear that she was getting no further than giving Simon the satisfaction of criticising her she said goodbye quietly and left. His evasiveness had left her seriously worried about what might happen at Whin Farm, and she hurried round to the office to warn Frances.

But the office was closed, and the phone rang and rang in an empty room. Gussie tried all afternoon, and in the evening she even rang Frances's hotel, but there was still no reply. In the end, she left a message asking Frances to call her urgently.

Frances never returned her call, and before Gussie could try and reach her again the next morning it was too late.

'FIRE! SETBACK FOR NEW COMPLEX' screamed the bill posters for the local newspaper as Gussie cycled into Bracklewick. Throwing down her bike, she ran into the newsagents to buy the paper with a sinking heart. Before she had even looked at the front page, she knew that it was about Whin Farm.

Simon would be delighted with the sensation he had created, she thought dully, staring down at a picture of

the blackened ruins of Whin Farm. The fire had destroyed all the outbuildings and had spread to the farmhouse. Now there was nothing left but smoking rubble.

Future Green had admitted responsibility quite openly.
'"Hunter Scott was going to destroy Whin Farm in a
much more insidious way,"' Simon was quoted as saying.
'"The ruins of Whin Farm are a symbol of what awaits
the countryside if we let developers like Scott have their
way."'

Gussie couldn't bear to read any more. Dropping the
paper back on to the counter, she left some coins and
went blindly back outside. She didn't want to read about
symbols; she wanted to know exactly how much damage
Simon had done.

When she got to Whin Farm, the ruins were still
smoking. She walked slowly across the ashes covering
the farmyard, remembering how Hunter had planned to
turn the tumbledown old buildings into the heart of a
thriving centre that everyone could enjoy. His image was
so clear that she could almost reach out and touch him.
How would he feel when he heard about the fire?

By some freak, the dilapidated wooden gate that led
to the meadow had escaped the flames. Gussie remembered how she had leant on it with Hunter and watched
the swallows swooping and diving with joy. Their nest
had been hidden under the eaves of the barn, where only
a blackened wall and the stubs of some smouldering
rafters remained.

Hoping against hope that they had survived, Gussie
peered up into the overhang, but her foot catching
against something in the ashes made her look down. The
nest had been dislodged by a cracking timber and had

fallen outside the fire, but the newly hatched birds hadn't stood a chance as they crashed to the ground.

The tears trickled down Gussie's cheeks as she crouched beside the pathetic bodies. It was all such a waste. Simon or Hunter would say that she was being sentimental, but deep down she knew that she was crying as much for herself as for the birds. She hadn't let herself cry about Hunter before, but the smoking ruins of the farm seemed an all too potent symbol of her own silly dreams. She had hoped against hope that he might come to love her, hoped that Frances was wrong and that he wasn't going to replace her after all, but she should have known all along that she was wasting her time dreaming of the impossible.

'I suppose you've come to gloat?'

The harsh voice behind her made Gussie spin round, her heart pumping with shock. 'Hunter!' She scrambled to her feet, the instinctive rush of joy at the sight of him fading as his words sank in. 'Gloat?' she echoed, bemused.

Hunter's dark features were white with suppressed anger, his eyes an icy grey as he met her startled gaze with contempt. 'I presume that you've come to inspect the results of another successful mission for Future Green?'

'You don't really think I had anything to do with this, do you?' Gussie demanded furiously, misery forgotten in a rush of outrage at the injustice of his accusation. The back of her mind remembered desolately how different things had been the last time they had been alone together. Then, he had held her close while she melted into his arms; now the air crackled with hostility as they glared at each other, both rigid with animosity.

'What else am I to think when I get back to hear that not only have you stopped coming into the office, but you've been seen holding hands with Simon Mansfield? Have you been reporting back to Future Green all along, with little tips as to how best to hurt the project?' A muscle jumped insistently in his cheek as he struggled unsuccessfully to control his rage. 'What a fool I was to be taken in by those great innocent eyes and that sanctimonious hypocrisy of yours!'

CHAPTER NINE

THE turbulent feelings that Gussie had kept suppressed for so long boiled over into uncontrollable fury, and she lashed out without thinking. 'You're a fine one to talk about hypocrisy!'

'Me?' Hunter was thrown momentarily off balance by her attack. Had he expected her to collapse into tears and admit everything? 'What do you mean?'

'You were the one who made a fool out of me!' Gussie brushed angrily at her wet cheeks, determined not to let him think she was crying because of him. 'I really fell for your line about making me an environmental consultant. How you and Frances must have laughed at my pathetic eagerness to do all that research for you, when all along you meant to get a professional in! Did you do it to keep me quiet, or was I just there to keep you amused?'

'Don't be ridiculous!' he snapped. 'It wasn't like that.'

'I think it was!' She turned away, hugging her arms defensively, and tried to get a grip on herself before her temper betrayed her into revealing too much. 'Oh, don't get me wrong,' she said in shaking voice. 'I don't blame you. I'm just as stupid and gullible as you took me for! I actually trusted you, actually thought you took me seriously!'

'I take you a lot more seriously now, believe me!' Hunter snarled. 'I don't quite see how burning down Whin Farm is supposed to benefit the environment, but you and your boyfriend are going to regret you ever thought up this particular publicity stunt! I'm going to have you both up for criminal damage.'

'I'm beginning to think Simon was right after all,' Gussie said, swinging back to face him with a vehement look. 'All you care about is claiming for damage to your property.' She gestured at the baby birds by her feet. 'It doesn't matter to you that there are three swallows here who never even had a chance to fly.'

'You should have thought of that before you went back to Future Green!'

'I didn't!' Gussie's voice rose in protest, and she pressed the heels of her hands against her eyes as her initial anger faded into flat despair that Hunter could think such a thing of her. 'I had nothing to do with the fire,' she said wearily.

'Then what were you doing holding hands with Simon?' he demanded.

'I wasn't holding hands with him.'

'Frances says you were. She saw you both looking intense yesterday morning, and since you hadn't been into the office she drew the obvious conclusion.'

Gussie's eyes flashed. 'If you're going to take everything Frances says as gospel, there doesn't seem much point in my explaining, but, for the record, I was *not* holding hands with Simon. I'd heard he was planning something destructive at Whin Farm, and I was trying to persuade him to forget the idea.'

Hunter was pacing around the farmyard, still too angry to stand still. 'If you're so innocent, why didn't you warn us?'

'I tried!' she cried. 'Ask Tony how many times I rang the office yesterday! Ask the hotel how many times I rang Frances's room! Better still, ask Frances why she didn't reply to my message asking her to call me urgently!'

'She must have thought that you were back with Future Green . . .' Hunter said. 'Couldn't you have tried to get hold of me instead?'

'How?' Gussie asked bitterly. He was ready enough to find excuses for Frances! 'You went off without letting me know where you were. Why should you? You didn't expect me to have anything important to say. I was just a joke, wasn't I? You're lucky I even tried to save your rotten project!' To her fury, she had started to cry again, and she brushed at the tears with her palms.

Hunter's slate-coloured eyes narrowed on her face with unnerving penetration. 'If you feel like that, why did you?'

'You needn't think I did it for you!' Gussie snapped, terrified that he would read the truth in her eyes. 'I was worried about what would happen to the wildlife, that's all.'

'Is that why you're crying? For three dead birds?'

'That's what happens when you get sentimental and obsessive!' Gussie scowled, willing the pathetic, angry, desolate tears to stop.

There was a pause. Hunter glared down at the ashes while he digested what she had said. His strong brows were drawn together and for the first time Gussie noticed the lines of exhaustion and bitterness that were carved into his cheeks.

'If you're not back with Future Green, why haven't you been into the office?' he asked at last. 'I thought you were committed to what you were doing.'

'I was committed until I realised that you weren't going to take any notice of anything I said!'

'That's not true——' he glowered, but she interrupted him before he could go on.

'Isn't it? Are you denying that you've been down to London to arrange for a professional consultant to come up?'

Hunter hesitated. 'No, I'm not denying that, but he wouldn't take over your job.'

'Then why didn't you tell me?'

'I was going to tell you when I took you home from the restaurant.' He looked away across the gate to the meadow. 'Unfortunately, I got a little distracted.'

Distracted? Gussie could feel the awareness of how they had kissed shimmering in the air between them. She had been enchanted, enraptured, blissfully in love, and he had been *distracted*!

Bitter knowledge of how near she had come to fooling herself sharpened her voice. 'I think I'd have preferred to hear about something that mattered to me than to be distracted like that!'

Hunter's face closed. 'Don't worry, it won't happen again!' His mouth was set in a grim line, and his eyes were cold. 'I ought to have known that you weren't interested in anything but your precious conservation work, but there's no need to make such a fuss about it.'

'You'd make a fuss if you were accused of arson and deceit and threatened with prosecution,' Gussie said, temper flaring comfortingly once more.

There was another taut silence while they bristled at each other, then Hunter exploded a sigh and raked his fingers through his hair. 'All right, I'm sorry! I suppose I should have known that you wouldn't have had anything to do with a fire like this, but when I got back to hear that you'd been seeing Simon...well, I lost my temper. I'm sorry.'

When Gussie still looked antagonistic, he went on between clenched teeth, 'I haven't done you out of a job— quite the opposite. Jim was very impressed by you and he's thinking of asking you to visit the existing leisure complexes they run and make suggestions about how things could be improved from a conservation point of view.'

Gussie was staggered. 'I...I don't know what to say.'

'I should think about it very seriously. Frankly, it's too good an opportunity for you to miss. You can't spend the rest of your life in Bracklewick, haranguing the shopkeepers about recycled carrier bags. You should be thinking about your future.'

He couldn't have made it plainer that he would have no part in it. Gussie looked at the sagging gate and thought about the future that stretched bleakly ahead of her without Hunter. Perhaps it would be easier to get over him away from the memories that linked him to Bracklewick?

'You don't have to decide immediately,' Hunter said stiffly. 'Jim thought you might like to meet some of his staff socially before you make up your mind. He suggested that his company's annual dinner-dance would be a good opportunity, so he's invited you to stay with him and his wife that night.' He paused. 'I offered to take you down to London. I'm invited to the dance anyway, so you can make a point and go on public transport, or drive down with me in comfort.'

Gussie hesitated. She hated grand occasions and never knew what to say to anyone, but Hunter was right. She *would* have to think about her future, and he was obviously keen to get rid of her.

'Well?' said Hunter. 'What are you dithering about?'

'I'm not dithering,' said Gussie, stung into a decision. 'I'll go.'

The more Gussie thought about the dinner-dance, the more she dreaded it. There would be lots of smart, sophisticated people there, and she would look drab and ridiculous in the green print dress she had bought to wear to Bellingham Hall. How could she ever have thought it was pretty? It was awful! More than anything else, she wanted to show Hunter that she was not the frumpy country mouse he thought her, but she simply couldn't afford to buy another dress. The prospect of looking silly in front of him made Gussie cross and miserable all week.

It was her mother who solved her dilemma. The night before the dance, she asked casually if Gussie would consider wearing an old dress of hers, and Gussie leapt at the idea. Anything would be better than that green thing!

'I wore this the night your father and I got engaged,' her mother said as she laid a flat box on the bed and lifted an old-fashioned russet dress out of the tissue paper. 'I couldn't bear to throw it away. It's shantung silk,' she went on, stroking the skirt with a reminiscent sigh. 'I was so proud of myself in it! Look, I even had my shoes covered in the same material to match.' She pulled a pair of court shoes out of the box and tried one next to Gussie's foot. 'My feet are a little bigger than yours, but if you pad the shoe out with an inner sole I'm sure you could manage for an evening.'

Gussie held the dress up against her in front of the mirror. It had a tight bodice with a rather full, stiff skirt, and the shawl collar was cut low over the shoulders, crossing elegantly over the cleavage. The dark silk gleamed in the light as she moved.

'It's old-fashioned, of course,' said her mother, eyeing her critically. 'But it would suit your colouring beautifully. I think you would get away with looking stylish and unusual, which is always better than looking fashionable anyway.'

Gussie didn't think that she could ever look stylish, but when she tried on the dress even she had to admit that it gave her an air of unfamiliar elegance, and she turned slowly in front of the mirror, trying not to wonder what Hunter would think of her.

The dress, shoes and a fine gossamer stole were packed carefully into Gussie's overnight bag when Hunter arrived to pick her up on the Friday morning. It was the first time she had seen him since he had found her in the dismal ruins of Whin Farm, and she was tense and nervous as he opened the car door for her.

'I'm not going to touch you!' Hunter snapped when Gussie brushed against him inadvertently and flinched at the electric jolt to her nerves.

'I'm not worried about *that*,' she said sharply, thrown off balance by the violence of her reaction.

'What *are* you worried about?' he asked, getting in beside her and slamming his own door shut. 'Compromising your precious principles by travelling all the way to London in a private car? You can cycle along behind if it makes you feel any better. It doesn't make any difference to me.'

'I'm not worried about anything,' Gussie said stiffly.

'Then why are you sitting there twanging away like a tuning-fork?' Hunter asked in a disagreeable tone. 'I don't fancy the thought of driving four hundred miles next to someone who's going to cower every time I change gear! For God's sake, relax!'

How could she relax with him shouting at her like that? Gussie stared huffily out of her window. He was a fine one to talk about relaxing, anyway! He looked as cross and tense as she felt. His expression was forbidding, the dark brows drawn over his nose and his jaw clamped, and he gripped the steering-wheel with ferocious concentration as he glared at the road ahead.

'I'm allowed to be apprehensive about meeting my prospective colleagues, aren't I?' she said at last. 'This could be an important evening for me. If I don't make the right impression, Jim might change his mind about offering me the job.'

'So you've decided that's what you want to do, have you?'

'Yes.' Gussie linked her hands together in her lap. All she wanted was to be with Hunter, but she could hardly tell him that. 'Naturally I want the job. You were the one who pointed out what a tremendous opportunity it would be for me.'

Hunter looked sour, but made no other comment, and Gussie lapsed into miserable silence. It was the worst journey of her life. The weather was filthy, the Friday traffic appalling and they had to crawl through nine sets of major roadworks, none of which improved Hunter's temper.

Gussie sat silently beside him and tried to think about anything other than the overwhelming need to reach across and touch him. She had a recurrent image of leaning over and resting her hand on his thigh, of seeing him turn and smile. The image was so vivid that she could practically feel the solid strength of his muscles tingling against her palm. She could imagine the gleaming laughter in his eyes so clearly that she would glance across at him, half expecting him to be smiling still, and her heart would contract when she saw the reality of his scowl instead.

By the time they eventually reached London, both of them were tired and snappy, frazzled by the long delays and incessant rain.

'It's too late to take you to Jim's house now,' Hunter said, sighing irritably as yet another traffic light changed to red just as they reached it. 'He lives south of the river and by the time we flog through the rush-hour they'll just be setting out. You'll just have to get changed at my flat, and Jim and his wife can take you home after the dance.'

Gussie had somehow expected Hunter to live in a plush house with gleaming coffee-tables and artful décor, and she was nonplussed when he pulled up outside a Chelsea warehouse. He led her up an iron staircase and threw open the door into a studio that even on that dreary summer evening seemed filled with light. A vast window opened on to a balcony that overlooked the river, and the effect of light and space was emphasised by the high ceiling and polished wooden floor. One long wall was covered with bookshelves, and a staircase spiralled up to a gallery bedroom.

'What a lovely room!' Gussie exclaimed involuntarily, stopping just inside the door.

Hunter shrugged. 'It's a convenient base for me, but I've been thinking of buying somewhere in the country.'

'In the country?' she echoed, surprised that he should want to sell such an attractive flat. 'Why?'

'You're not the only one entitled to live in the country,' he snapped before recovering himself with an effort. 'I haven't decided yet, anyway.' Before Gussie could ask any more questions, he pointed up to the gallery. 'You'll find a bathroom up there. I suggest you go and get changed while I ring Jim and explain that we'll meet them there.'

For Gussie, there was an unbearable intimacy about laying her dress out on Hunter's bed, standing naked under Hunter's shower, pinching some of Hunter's toothpaste when she realised that she had forgotten her own... Impossible not to remember how he had kissed her and to wish and wish that things could have been different.

She stepped into the dress and slid the zip up her back, and even such a mundane action made her shiver with the thought of how it would have been if it had been Hunter's fingers brushing against her skin, Hunter's hands at the nape of her neck. Her mother had persuaded her to accept a lipstick once she had checked that it had been tested without cruelty to animals, and as Gussie leant towards the mirror to put it on the memory of Hunter's mouth was suddenly so sharp and vivid that she straightened with a gasp.

If only she hadn't started thinking like this! Gussie's fingers trembled as she fixed her grandmother's amber earrings into her ears. She had been doing so well at convincing herself that her feelings for Hunter had been destroyed by the argument they had had. Now was not the time for her body to start burning with awareness again. There was no point in standing up here, aching for his touch, when he had made it so clear that she could never be anything more than a distraction.

Her reflection gazed back at her with eyes that were wide and dark with longing. The russet tones of the dress caught the autumnal tones in her hair and flattered the warm sheen of her skin. Gussie fiddled with the neckline of the dress. She wasn't used to wearing anything cut so low and she was very conscious of her bare shoulders and the shadow of her cleavage. Hastily, she draped the gossamer shawl around her. She felt less vulnerable like that, unaware of how her pale skin gleamed seductively through the fine material.

Taking a deep breath, Gussie walked over to the top of the stairs. She was stupidly shy of showing herself to Hunter in this guise and desperately afraid that he would read the sensuousness in her eyes.

She peered over the gallery. Hunter was standing in front of the big window, hands thrust deep into his pockets as he watched the rain sliding down the glass. He had loosened his tie and his shoulders were slumped as if he was very tired. A piano concerto played softly in the background. Gussie thought that she had never seen him look so lonely. She longed to go and stand beside him, to put her arms around him and rest her cheek against his heart.

As if suddenly aware of her gaze, Hunter turned to see her hesitating at the top of the stairs, her expression unguarded and her cloudy hair glinting in the light. He stared up at her, his eyes widening in stunned surprise at the transformation from jeans and sweatshirt to this simple elegance, and stepped forward as she came carefully down the stairs. Her skirts swayed against her bare legs and her hair fell forward to hide her face as she watched her feet, but when she reached the last step she looked up at Hunter.

He hadn't said a word. He was just watching her with an unreadable expression which none the less tightened Gussie's chest and set her pulse pounding slowly and uncomfortably. As the silence lengthened, she moved awkwardly away and cleared her throat.

'I'm sorry if I've kept you waiting,' she said at last in a stilted voice that sounded strange to her own ears.

'It doesn't matter,' Hunter said with equally stiff politeness. 'You obviously want to make an effort for your potential new boss and colleagues.'

Gussie had been so preoccupied with her feelings for Hunter that she had forgotten about the job Jim was going to offer her. Hunter obviously hadn't. This evening was business for him.

'Yes,' she said dully.

Hunter made as if to step towards her, but he checked himself, and headed for the stairs instead. 'I'll just go and change,' he said with an odd edge of bitterness to his voice. 'I won't keep you long. I've booked a taxi for half-past seven.'

When he reappeared, he was freshly shaved and the severe black of the bow-tie against the dazzling whiteness of his shirt lent him an austere elegance that did nothing to diminish the air of tough competence that was so much part of him. He looked devastatingly attractive, and Gussie's mouth dried at the sight of him.

He came down the stairs quickly, shrugging himself into his jacket as he glanced at his watch. 'Half-past seven—I hope the taxi's on time or we'll be late.' He was trying to fasten his cuff-links, but gave up with an exclamation of disgust and held out his arm. 'Can you give me a hand, Gussie? These things are so damn fiddly!'

Gussie pushed her hair nervously behind her ears and bent her head over his wrist. She stared down at his hand as if she had never seen one before. The clean, square-cut nails, the dark hairs beneath the stiff white cuff and the tiny stitching round the buttonholes, the grooves on his knuckles, even the pores of his skin stood out with unnatural clarity. At the edge of her vision, she could see him breathing, and her fingers shook as she fumbled with the cuff-links.

'There.' She pushed the last one through its hole with relief and glanced up, surprising a look in the slate-blue eyes that made the earth drop beneath her feet. Unaware of her fingers still at his cuff, they stared at each other while the silence strummed with an almost tangible tension that tightened and tightened until, just when Gussie thought it must snap, the jarring noise of the doorbuzzer broke the spell and she snatched her hand away from his wrist as if she had been stung.

'Here's the taxi,' Hunter said unnecessarily. His voice sounded a little uneven as he turned abruptly away, buttoning his jacket and tugging the sleeves into place.

They were very careful not to touch in the taxi. They sat as far away from each other as possible, and stared out of their windows without speaking. Later, Gussie could remember nothing about the trip except the leathery smell of the upholstery and the faint swish of the taxi's tyres on the wet roads and Hunter's silently reverberating presence.

The dinner was held in the one of the grander hotels, and Jim Barker was an excellent host, but for Gussie the evening was a blur of names and faces. She talked and danced and smiled, and tried not to notice that Hunter was the only man at the table not to ask her to dance.

The band changed to slower music as she came back to the table, breathless from an energetic dance with Jim's chief accountant, and wild hope leapt in her breast as she saw Hunter get to his feet. Was he going to ask her to dance after all? But at that moment one of the other men at the table claimed her noisily for the next dance, and when Gussie saw that Hunter was in any case heading for a completely different table she smiled brightly and accepted.

She kept the same bright, artificial smile pinned to her face throughout the dance. It faltered only once, when she saw that Hunter was dancing with Frances, who wore a provocatively cut long sheath dress, flounced at the hem and ruffled below bare shoulders, in a brilliant red that emphasised her dramatic looks.

Watching her swaying close to Hunter, Gussie finally gave up. She had always known that Frances was his kind of woman, a suitable successor to Imogen without Imogen's obsession with her work. How could she ever have allowed herself to forget it? All the doubts and suspicions that had wavered at the look in Hunter's eyes as she'd fastened his cuff came rolling back. It was hopeless; it had always been hopeless. All she could do now was put Hunter out of her mind for good and think about the job Jim had offered her. She had the chance of a career with a real impact on the environment. That would have to be enough.

She danced indefatigably for the rest of the evening, and managed to ignore Hunter until, right at the end of the dance, Jim took her back to the table. Hunter was there, looking dark and austere, and talking to Jim's wife, Mary. Jim hailed them merrily.

'Come along, Mary, I hope you've saved the last dance for me! It's a nice slow one for us. Hunter, you've been watching Gussie all evening; now's your chance to grab her before somebody else jumps in.'

He twirled his wife off, leaving Hunter and Gussie awkwardly alone.

'Shall we?' Hunter asked after a moment. He held out his hand, and Gussie took it, miserably aware that he would have avoided her if Jim hadn't left him with no choice. His palm burnt against hers where they touched.

She stared at a point somewhere past his ear as he held her stiffly, one hand grasping hers, the other against the small of her back. They tried to keep a space between their bodies, but the floor was crowded, and they kept getting jostled together, only to pull themselves apart immediately.

Gradually, though, the slow, seductive beat of the band wound itself round them, dissolving the tension until the noisy, crowded room receded, leaving the two of them alone with the music. No words were spoken as imperceptibly, irresistibly they drew together. Gussie tried to remind herself of just why she had to put any thought of Hunter from her mind, but her body, with a will of its own, relaxed in spite of all her strictures. Hunter's hand drifted slowly up and down her spine, pulling her closer by infinitesimal degrees until, with a tiny sigh of pleasure, she gave in at last and leant against him. Her face rested in the hollow between his neck and the broad shoulder, her lips a breath away from the pulse beating below his ear. She could smell the faint tang of his after-shave and feel the strong, steady beat of his heart.

His hand was warm and insistent on her back. Gussie quivered beneath his touch, curling herself around him, all thought of past or future abandoned to the sheer joy of being close to him.

Hunter laid his cheek against her hair and his arm tightened around her as he brought their entwined hands close to his chest. His lips brushed her hair and drifted down to her temple, but before she could tilt her face to meet his kiss the music stopped with a flourish and the lights came up.

Gussie could have wept with frustration. Hunter's hold slackened as they found themselves surrounded by rev-ellers, and the next moment they were swept apart by a whooping crowd bent on a spirited, if inaccurate ren-dition of 'Auld lang syne'. Streamers fell from the ceiling as Gussie was pushed back to form part of the huge circle and her hands were ruthlessly grabbed across her body by grinning dancers.

Dazed by the abrupt change of mood, Gussie looked wildly around for Hunter, but the dance-floor was now a seething, jovial mass of people and she had no choice but to let her arms be pumped up and down. There were cheers and whistles as the song came to a noisy end, and Gussie was thoroughly kissed by a number of strangers before she managed to struggle to the edge of the dance-floor.

Stopping to catch her breath, she found herself standing next to Frances, who looked her up and down appraisingly. 'You should dress up more often,' she said in her cool, faintly condescending voice. 'I didn't recognise you at first. I had to ask who the girl was clinging to Hunter like a limpet.'

The light amusement in Frances's voice stripped the last lingering magic from Gussie's dance with Hunter and her colour rose. Was that how she had appeared? Besotted and clinging to a man who had been practically forced to ask her to dance? Had he been rolling his eyes at Frances over her shoulder, embarrassed by her infatuation? Frances would not have been so amused if Hunter had looked as if he were taking her seriously.

'Has he told you yet?' Frances asked and Gussie stared blankly at her.

'Told me what?'

'About Brazil?' When Gussie shook her head dumbly, Frances shrugged. 'I suppose he's waiting for the right moment to say goodbye. He wouldn't want a scene here. I dare say he'll break it to you on the way home.'

Gussie found her voice. 'Break *what* to me?'

'He's not going back to Northumberland. The chance of a big project has come up in Brazil, and he'll have to fly out next week. One of his deputies can easily take over Whin Farm; Hunter wasn't planning to stay up there much longer anyway. You probably knew that.'

'Yes,' said Gussie dully.

This, then, was it. She would say goodbye to Hunter tonight, and she would never see him again.

'Are you going to Brazil too?' she forced herself to ask Frances.

'Of course.' Frances smiled smugly. 'Hunter and I are a team.'

Gussie made her way blindly back to the table, where everyone was beginning the long process of saying goodnight, which somehow got diverted into new conversations. Hunter was there, making an unconvincing effort to appear interested in what the chief accountant's wife was saying to him, but his head jerked round at Gussie's approach.

Avoiding his eye, she plunged into desperate conversation with Mary Barker. Hunter managed to extricate himself, and began pushing towards her through the group. He had almost reached her when Mary's attention was diverted by a couple ready to leave, and Gussie was left stranded. Unable to bear the prospect of Hunter saying goodbye, she turned her back deliberately and began talking brightly to someone else just as Hunter reached her side.

'Gussie!' he said between his teeth, but she ignored him. She could feel his eyes boring into her back and expected any second to feel herself swung round, but Jim Barker saved her.

'What's all this I hear about Brazil?' he asked jovially, clapping his hand on Hunter's shoulder, and Hunter was forced into polite explanations.

A shutter clanged Gussie's heart shut. Hunter's trip to Brazil was obviously common knowledge. She was the only person he hadn't bothered to tell. If he was expecting her to burst into tears when he finally got round to telling her, he could think again. She would show that she couldn't care less *where* he was going!

She edged her way further round the table, moving from conversation to conversation. Hunter followed her, always just too late to prevent her slipping into yet another group, until at last his patience snapped.

'Excuse me,' he grated, shouldering aside the chief accountant and grabbing Gussie by the wrist. 'I just need a word with Gussie.' Ignoring the surprised looks, he dragged her over to one of the glass doors that lined the ballroom, pushed her through the curtains on to the balcony and yanked her into his arms.

CHAPTER TEN

HELPLESS, Gussie was slammed against his rock-hard body. Her eyes were wide with alarm as he jerked up her chin and she tried to pull away, but he was too strong for her. With a smothered exclamation, he captured her parted lips with his mouth as if to punish her for his anger and frustration.

Gussie struggled, but his mouth was fiercely possessive, and a treacherous excitement shuddered through her as desire coiled insidiously around them.

'What are you playing at, Gussie?' he demanded hoarsely, burning kisses down her throat. His hands were hard and urgent, his mouth like fire against her skin. 'One minute you're warm and soft in my arms, and the next you won't even look at me! You want this as much as I did, I know you do.'

'No,' Gussie whispered, turning her head from side to side, but her senses screamed that she was lying.

'Yes.' Hunter's lips travelled slowly back to her mouth, and when he kissed her again she could no longer deny the spiralling excitement that spun her out of her futile attempts to resist and abandoned her to the intoxicating delight of his embrace.

Her arms slipped beneath his jacket and she spread her hands over his back, luxuriating in the feel of the steely muscles beneath the fine material of his shirt. Their tongues tasted and twined, and Hunter's fingers tangled in her hair as he pushed her back against the wall, deepening the kiss.

When at last his lips left hers to trace scorching patterns of desire along the pure line of her clavicle and over her bare shoulders, Gussie murmured low in her throat. She was enthralled, bewitched by his caresses, caught up in a web of longing that held her defenceless against a growing throb of need.

Hunter's hands moved hungrily over her slender curves as his mouth reached the soft shadow between her breasts. His tongue flickered against her skin and Gussie gasped involuntarily, shaken by the jolt of feeling that surged through her.

'You see,' he said in low, ragged voice. 'You do want me. Stay with me tonight, Gussie,' he urged, as his lips continued their devastating exploration. 'Come home with me now. Jim will understand.'

With an immense effort, Gussie shook her head, pushing aside the demons of temptation that whispered to her body of the ecstasy that a night with Hunter would bring. But it would just be for a night, it would just delay their goodbye by a few hours. How could it mean anything to Hunter? She had only ever been a passing amusement for him. His sights were firmly set on Brazil and there would be no place for her, not when he had Frances there.

'Why not?' Hunter lifted his head to look down into her eyes, but she turned her face away.

'I don't feel like being a distraction tonight.'

'A distraction?' He stared at her incredulously for a moment. 'You've been that all right, ever since I met you, but do you really think that's all you are?' Half smiling, he let his fingers drift along the neckline of her dress, watching her skin quiver with awareness, until she slapped his hand away.

'You've made it obvious enough,' she said with bitterness. 'I suppose you thought I might be distracted by spending the night with you before you swan off to Brazil? Were you even going to tell me you were going, or was that little piece of news supposed to "distract" me when I got back to Bracklewick?'

His smile had vanished. 'Who told you about Brazil?'

'Does it matter?' she challenged him.

'I wanted to tell you myself,' he said heavily.

'Oh, really? Well, you needn't put yourself to the bother now. I don't have the slightest interest in where you go or what you do or whom you distract yourself with!'

Hunter stepped back as if she had struck him. 'Do you mean that?'

'Yes.' Gussie was so miserable that she just wanted to be left alone. 'Yes, I do. I don't care if I never see you again.'

'You didn't kiss me as if you didn't care,' he said tightly.

'Oh, you don't want to read too much into a kiss,' she said with a brittle smile. 'I've learnt not to.'

'Gussie——' Hunter began, stretching out his hand, but Gussie couldn't bear any more.

'Jim and Mary will be looking for me. I'd better go,' she said on a gasp, and, whirling round, she stumbled back into the ballroom before he could stop her.

To her relief, Jim and Mary were ready to leave. 'We'll just say goodbye to Hunter,' Jim said, hailing him as he appeared in his turn from the balcony, grim-faced.

'I—I've said goodbye,' Gussie said, her throat so tight with misery that she could hardly speak. 'I'll go and collect my bag from the cloakroom.' She hurried off before Hunter reached them, and when she came back he had gone.

Gone. Gone. Gone.

In a daze of wretched exhaustion, Gussie let Jim and Mary take her home. She supposed she must have thanked them as they showed her into a comfortable guest room and told her to sleep as long as she liked in the morning, but nothing seemed to matter apart from the fact that she would never see Hunter again.

She lay dry-eyed on the bed and stared at the ceiling, torturing herself with thoughts of how different things might have been if she had gone back with Hunter after all. Her body ached as she imagined running her hands over his hardness, feeling his lips against her skin, discovering together the breathtaking heights of passion...

Gussie rolled over and buried her face in the pillow. It was too late now.

In spite of her exhaustion, she couldn't sleep, and in the morning she looked gaunt and ravaged. Jim put her appearance down to the late night, but he was concerned to hear that she planned to take the first coach up to Northumberland.

'But I thought Hunter was going to drive you home?'

Gussie concentrated on her toast. She wasn't hungry, and it took an enormous effort to chew. 'He can't really spare the time before he goes to Brazil,' she said, surprised at how calm she sounded.

'Ah, yes...he's off next week, isn't he?' Jim leant forward conspiratorially. 'A little bird told me that he's making plans for a certain someone to accompany him...'

Gussie thought of Frances and nodded desolately.

'Of course, it's a shame to combine it with business,' Jim went on, buttering his toast with a lavish disregard for cholesterol. 'But I dare say there'll be plenty of time for the honeymoon!'

'Honeymoon?' Gussie croaked and Jim looked guilty.

'Oh, is it supposed to be a secret? I thought from what Hunter said...' He trailed off under a quelling look from his wife, and hastened to change the subject. 'Would you like a lift to the coach station?'

Hunter was going to marry Frances. The knowledge scraped at Gussie's raw heart all the long, dreary way back up to Northumberland. Knowing that he didn't love her was bad enough, but the thought of him loving Frances was far, far worse.

Margaret Blake took one look at Gussie's face when she got home and asked no questions. Gussie never knew whether she said anything to her brothers, but they were unusually gentle with her over the next few days, and Tony was equally understanding.

'You're not yourself,' he said firmly. 'We can manage perfectly well without you for a few days. You go and get some colour back in your cheeks.'

Gussie had never known that misery could be like this. Her body ached with unhappiness and every movement was a physical effort, but she spent long hours walking over the moors with Ruby and Angus, trying to break out of the numb despair that enveloped her. Memories of Hunter beat at her: the turn of his head, the line of his jaw, the touch of his mouth. It made no difference to remind herself how little she had meant to him; she still loved him.

She wished she could cry, but all she could do was hurt. When things got too bad, she went back to the Whin woods like a wounded animal, and lay for long hours in the hide, just as she had when she was a child, letting the quietness of the woods settle round her.

She was dully calculating that she had survived four and a half days without Hunter and wondering how long it would be before his memory released its steel claws from her heart, when the sound of someone approaching through the wood made her flatten herself against the wooden planks. She didn't want to talk to anyone; if she lay very still, he or she might pass on without even noticing her perch in the tree. When the rustling stopped, she knew that the intruder had stepped into the clearing from the undergrowth, but the silence that followed went on for so long that she raised her head cautiously to see where whoever it was had gone. The clearing was empty.

'I'm here,' said a voice directly beneath her, and Gussie caught her breath in shock as she scrambled into a sitting position. Hunter was standing at the foot of the tree. 'Can I come up?'

Without waiting for an answer, he climbed up to the hide and sat down beside her. 'Hello,' he said.

Gussie's heart was slamming against her ribs. She stared at him with incredulous golden eyes, certain that if she touched him he would disappear in a puff of smoke. It would be too cruel if he wasn't real!

He *looked* real. He looked just as she had remembered so vividly, right down to the way the dark hair grew at his temples. The corner of his mobile mouth curled, as if he was about to break into a smile, and his slate-blue eyes were warmer than she had ever seen them. The grim, angry man she had last seen might never have been.

His mouth twitched at her disbelieving scrutiny. 'You seem surprised to see me.'

Gussie looked hurriedly away. 'I thought you'd be on the way to Brazil by now,' she said with an effort, fixing her eyes on the badgers' set.

'I don't leave until Saturday.' Hunter paused. 'You didn't really think I'd go without saying goodbye, did you?'

There was a long silence, then Gussie turned her head slowly to look at him again, her eyes huge and wary. 'I thought we said goodbye in London.'

'That damned dinner-dance!' Hunter said with feeling. He watched a wood-pigeon settle in a tree on the far side of the clearing. 'It was impossible trying to talk to you there. Whenever I tried to get close to you, you were surrounded by men and I was damned if I was going to stand in a queue to dance with you. And then when I did get you alone I made a mess of it. I never had a chance to explain about Brazil.'

'Frances told me about it,' Gussie said tonelessly. 'There was no need for you to explain anything.'

'Did she tell you how important the project is?'

Gussie shook her head. She didn't want to hear about what Hunter and Frances would be doing together.

'If we win the contract, we'll be developing a tourist resort in the upper reaches of the Amazon.' Hunter seemed determined to tell her anyway. 'The idea is to allow people access to the rainforest so that they learn to appreciate its true value, but, of course, the damage to the immediate environment has to be minimal.' He glanced at her set face. 'You'd love it.'

'Perhaps,' she said, tight-lipped. Did he think it was funny to dangle her dream in front of her, only to snatch it away? *She* wouldn't be going to Brazil. It was Frances who would gaze up into the forest canopy, Frances who would watch the birds swooping over the Amazon and hear the insects whirr in their millions, Frances who would turn to Hunter with starry eyes.

Hunter reached into his jacket pocket and drew out a folded piece of paper. 'You might be interested to see the itinerary,' he said, rubbing salt into the wound.

Gussie felt like tearing his itinerary into tiny pieces, but she took the paper and glanced down it. Her heart twisted when she saw the heading: 'Mr and Mrs Scott'. So Jim had been right. Hunter and Frances were to be married. They were booked to fly to Rio de Janeiro on Saturday and from there to Manaus. After that, they were to take a private boat to explore up river. Hunter and the Amazon...it was a dream so perfect, and so impossible, that Gussie couldn't bear to imagine it.

'Very interesting,' she said in a flat voice, handing the itinerary back with a show of disinterest. 'I'm sure you'll enjoy yourselves, even if you do have to mix business with pleasure.'

'I'm sure we will.' Gussie could hear the smile in his voice, but she couldn't bear to look at him and see the happiness in his eyes. 'Of course, the real honeymoon will have to wait for three or four weeks. I've left the tickets open-ended, so that we can go anywhere after business is over. Look.'

Why was he torturing her like this? Gussie took the plane ticket he handed her and stared down at it blindly. He had folded the ticket back so that she could see the details, but the letters danced in front of her eyes. Blinking back the tears, she stared down at the blurry name until at last she managed to focus on 'Scott, Mrs A.'... Mrs *A.*?

Gussie closed her eyes, certain that they were colluding with Hunter in playing a cruel trick again, but when she looked again the A was still there. She swallowed. Hunter was watching her face, and very, very slowly she lifted her head to meet his eyes.

'A?' she whispered.

'A for Augusta,' he said gently.

Gussie looked down at the ticket, and then back at Hunter. 'Me?'

'You're the only Augusta I know.'

'But...but I thought you were going to marry Frances,' she said, still unable to take it in.

Hunter took the ticket firmly from her nerveless hand and tucked it back in his pocket. 'Why would I want to marry Frances when I'm desperately in love with you?' he asked in a conversational tone.

'You can't be in love with me,' Gussie said without thinking, and Hunter smiled as he took both her hands in his.

'Well, I'm sorry, but I am.' His voice deepened. 'So much in love that I've had to drive all the way up from London and clamber up a tree just to find out if you really meant it when you said you didn't care about me.'

His fingers tightened around hers. 'I was so sure you did that I bought you a ring when I went down to Jim's meeting. I was going to ask you to marry me then, but when I got back to Bracklewick, ready to throw myself at your feet, I heard that you'd been seen holding hands with Simon Mansfield. I was wild with jealousy and far more bitter about that than about the fire. You were so angry that I wondered if I'd been wrong after all; that's when I made that stupid remark about getting distracted by kissing you.'

He smiled down into her wondering face. 'Not that it was untrue! Ever since that first time I kissed you, I thought about nothing else but what it would be like to kiss you again. I tried not to, of course. I knew I'd have to leave Bracklewick eventually, and you loved the country so much, I couldn't imagine you ever giving it up to come and live with me in a city. I thought of all the reasons why it wouldn't be a good idea to get involved with you, but it didn't stop me falling in love with you. I'd never met a girl with such shining eyes and such shining beliefs before.'

Gussie's fingers curled around his, hardly daring to hope that this might not be just a glorious dream. 'You told me I was obsessive,' she reminded him. 'You said I was like Imogen and you never wanted anything to do with obsessive women again.'

'You're not like Imogen,' Hunter said seriously. 'You couldn't be more different. Imogen's obsession was centred on herself; you *care*.' He gave a slightly shamefaced grin. 'The truth is that I was jealous of how much you cared about the countryside. I wanted you to care that way about me.' He looked deep into her eyes. 'Well? Could you love me as I am, or do I have to declare myself an endangered species?'

Gussie's eyes were like stars as she smiled at him. 'I'm very much afraid I could get obsessive about you,' she admitted.

Hunter released her hands to draw her closer and the kiss they shared was dizzyingly sweet and tender with unspoken promise. It went on and on, and they sank back on to the floor of the hide, careless of the hard, uncomfortable planks or the long drop to the ground.

'Well?' she teased him, rolling on top of him to drop soft kisses along his jaw as she echoed his question. 'Do you believe I love you now?'

'I'm not quite sure,' Hunter mumbled, taking her head between his hands and pulling her face down to his. 'I need more convincing!'

They were breathless and smiling when they broke apart. 'We're disturbing the badgers,' he said, and Gussie laughed. She rested her head happily on his shoulder and his arms tightened about her. They lay together and looked up into the branches while the sunlight filtering through the leaves threw green shade over their skin.

'I can't believe you really love me,' she said, kissing his ear to reassure herself. 'I was so sure you were going to marry Frances. *She* knew that I was in love with you. She told me that I was being an embarrassing nuisance. That's why I stopped going into the office.'

'It's lucky for Frances that she's so good at her job,' Hunter said grimly. 'She's got a nasty habit of interfering in things that don't concern her, but I've always kept her on because she's an exceptional publicist, and good PR is essential in our line of work. In fact, she's so valuable that I think she'd better deal with things in London while we're in Brazil.'

'She said she was going to Brazil with you,' Gussie said. 'So when Jim started talking about honeymoons, I assumed that he meant you and Frances.'

'Yes, he told me you reacted rather strangely.' Hunter's hands drifted in luxurious possession over her body. 'He guessed how I felt about you, and I told him that I wanted to take you to Brazil with me. He had mentioned offering you a job before then, and I'm afraid I rather used it as a ruse to get you down to London. I thought that it might be easier to talk to you away from Bracklewick, but I got my come-uppance when you started showing a real interest in the job! That wasn't what I had in mind at all, so I asked Jim if he'd mind not offering you anything definite until I'd spoken to you about Brazil.

'You were so distant on that wretched drive down that I decided it wasn't worth saying anything then. I was convinced that I'd made a mess of everything by shouting at you about Simon and the fire. I even began to wonder if I'd read more into your kisses than I should have done.' He sighed and pulled Gussie closer into his arms. 'No wonder I was in such a filthy mood! And then, when we got to the studio, you changed and suddenly there was this beautiful, stylish girl standing before me. I still don't know how I stopped myself from kissing you there and then, but I was more and more unsure of how you really felt. As soon as we danced, though, and I held you in my arms, I knew, or thought I knew, that you were mine. You were so different from all the other girls in the room, so fresh and natural, and I was so proud of you,' he said. 'I was determined to ask you to marry me then, but we were separated by all those bloody revellers, and when I found you all your prickles were out again. I was so frustrated that I lost my head and my temper and dragged you outside.'

Hunter stroked Gussie's hair with a rueful smile. 'You know how far that got me! I asked Jim if I could come round and see you the next morning when we'd both had a chance to calm down, but by the time I got there you'd gone. I was sure then that you'd meant what you'd said about disliking me, but Jim told me not to be such a damn fool. He said it was perfectly obvious that you loved me and that if I let you go I'd be an even bigger fool.

'Time was running out, so I fixed up all the arrangements for Brazil and got a marriage licence. Whenever my courage faltered, I'd think about what Jim had said and remember how you kissed me.' Rolling her beneath him, he kissed her again and Gussie wound her arms around his neck and kissed him back. 'Like that,' he said with a smile. 'I didn't get it all sorted out till this morning, and I got straight in the car. I hope you realise how much petrol I've wasted chasing around the country after you! If we run out of oil in the next few years, I'll know who to blame,' he teased.

'How did you find me?' asked Gussie, sighing with happiness.

'I went to the wine bar first of all, and derived some consolation from Tony, who said he'd never seen you looking so desperate. He sent me to your house, where I saw your mother. She was rather cross with me at first. She said I'd broken your heart, but when I told her what a mess I'd made of everything she relented and said it was high time we both stopped being so silly. She said she didn't know where you'd gone, but I remembered what you'd told me about coming to the hide whenever you felt miserable, so I came straight here.' He ran a finger tenderly down her cheek. 'It wasn't hard to spot you. This isn't much of a hide. I don't know about the badgers, but I saw you straight away! The sun through the trees just caught your hair and it was so bright and shining that I knew it could only be you.' He rubbed a lock through his fingers. 'You'll have to have better camouflage in the Amazon!'

He sat up, pulling Gussie with him. 'Talking of the Amazon, you haven't said whether you'll marry me yet.'

'You haven't asked me yet,' she pointed out mischievously.

Hunter brushed a leaf off her shoulder. 'Gussie, darling, will you marry me?'

'Yes,' said Gussie simply, and he kissed her, a deep, true kiss that pledged a lifetime of love.

'Do you mind getting married straight away?' he asked as he released her. 'I might have to spend several months in Brazil, and I can't face them without you.' When she shook her head, smiling, he searched in his pockets for the ring.

It was a simple topaz surrounded by seed-pearls. Delighted, Gussie turned her hand this way and that so that the topaz caught the light, and the colours changed, deep and clear.

'The topaz reminded me of your eyes,' Hunter said. 'I bought it as soon as I saw it, and it was only later that I remembered you'd probably protest about the poor oysters being stripped of their pearls!'

'I think I can live with my conscience,' Gussie said, laying her hand tenderly against his cheek.

Much later, they walked back through the woods. Gussie's heart was soaring with happiness and the trees seemed to shimmer through an enchanted haze. It was impossible to believe that anywhere—even the Amazon— could be as beautiful as Whin Woods at that moment.

'What will happen to Whin Farm?' she asked as they reached the road and stood for a moment looking across the gate at the meadow which glowed golden in the slanting evening light.

'I've appointed my best deputy to look after the project,' said Hunter. 'He won't let anything spoil your woods, Gussie.' He squeezed her hand. 'Whin Farm will survive without you, but I won't. Besides,' he grinned, 'where you're going, there'll be more than enough to keep you occupied. You can save the rainforest single-handed after all, as long as you keep some of your passion for me at the end of the day.'

He glanced around him. 'Do you realise that this is exactly where we first met? I think I've loved you ever since you jumped out at me, brandishing that ridiculous placard. Your eyes were shining then, too.' He touched them tenderly with his finger. 'I hope you're not planning any more protests against me?'

'No.' Gussie put her arms round him and rested her cheek against the miraculously steady beat of his heart. 'I'm on your side now.'

HARLEQUIN ROMANCE®

brings you

Romances that take the family to heart!

A FAMILY CLOSENESS by Emma Richmond

If Davina's fiancé hadn't run off with her best friend, she wouldn't have got involved with Joel Gilman. And now, four years after their disastrous encounter, it seemed that time hadn't dulled their mutual attraction! But Joel had a new woman in his life now—his young daughter, Ammy. And when he asked her to look after the little girl, Davina had a temporary chance to experience what might have been—and what she'd always wanted....

Coming next month, from the bestselling author of
.MORE THAN A DREAM!

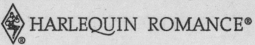

HARLEQUIN®

Don't miss these Harlequin favorites by some of our most distinguished authors!
And now, you can receive a discount by ordering two or more titles!

HT #25559	JUST ANOTHER PRETTY FACE by Candace Schuler	$2.99	☐
HT #25616	THE BOUNTY HUNTER by Vicki Lewis Thompson	$2.99 U.S./$3.50 CAN.	☐
HP #11667	THE SPANISH CONNECTION by Kay Thorpe	$2.99 U.S./$3.50 CAN.	☐
HP #11701	PRACTISE TO DECEIVE by Sally Wentworth	$2.99 U.S./$3.50 CAN.	☐
HR #03268	THE BAD PENNY by Susan Fox	$2.99	☐
HR #03340	THE NUTCRACKER PRINCE by Rebecca Winters	$2.99 U.S./$3.50 CAN.	☐
HS #70540	FOR THE LOVE OF IVY by Barbara Kaye	$3.39	☐
HS #70596	DANCING IN THE DARK by Lynn Erickson	$3.50	☐
HI #22196	CHILD'S PLAY by Bethany Campbell	$2.89	☐
HI #22304	BEARING GIFTS by Aimée Thurlo	$2.99 U.S./$3.50 CAN.	☐
HAR #16538	KISSED BY THE SEA by Rebecca Flanders	$3.50 U.S./$3.99 CAN.	☐
HAR #16553	THE MARRYING TYPE by Judith Arnold	$3.50 U.S./$3.99 CAN.	☐
HH #28847	DESIRE MY LOVE by Miranda Jarrett	$3.99 U.S./$4.50 CAN	☐
HH #28848	VOWS by Margaret Moore	$3.99 U.S./$4.50 CAN.	☐

(limited quantities available on certain titles)

	AMOUNT	$	
DEDUCT:	**10% DISCOUNT FOR 2+ BOOKS**	$	
	POSTAGE & HANDLING ($1.00 for one book, 50¢ for each additional)	$	
	APPLICABLE TAXES*	$	
	<u>**TOTAL PAYABLE**</u> (check or money order—please do not send cash)	$	

To order, complete this form and send it, along with a check or money order for the
total above, payable to Harlequin Books, to: **In the U.S.:** 3010 Walden Avenue,
P.O. Box 9047, Buffalo, NY 14269-9047; **In Canada:** P.O. Box 613, Fort Erie, Ontario,
L2A 5X3.

Name: _____

Address: _____ City: _____

State/Prov.: _____ Zip/Postal Code: _____

*New York residents remit applicable sales taxes.
 Canadian residents remit applicable GST and provincial taxes.   HBACK-JS2

FLYAWAY VACATION SWEEPSTAKES!

This month's destination:

Glamorous LAS VEGAS!

Are you the lucky person who will win a free trip to Las Vegas? Think how much fun it would be to visit world-famous casinos... to see star-studded shows...to enjoy round-the-clock action in the city that never sleeps!

The facing page contains two Official Entry Coupons, as does each of the other books you received this shipment. Complete and return all the entry coupons— **the more times you enter, the better your chances of winning!**

Then keep your fingers crossed, because you'll find out by August 15, 1995 if you're the winner! If you are, here's what you'll get:

- Round-trip airfare for two to exciting Las Vegas!
- 4 days/3 nights at a fabulous first-class hotel!
- $500.00 pocket money for meals and entertainment!

Remember: The more times you enter, the better your chances of winning!*

FLYAWAY VACATION
SWEEPSTAKES

OFFICIAL ENTRY COUPON

This entry must be received by: JULY 30, 1995
This month's winner will be notified by: AUGUST 15, 1995
Trip must be taken between: SEPTEMBER 30, 1995-SEPTEMBER 30, 1996

YES, I want to win a vacation for two in Las Vegas. I understand the prize includes round-trip airfare, first-class hotel and $500.00 spending money. Please let me know if I'm the winner!

Name_____

Address _____ Apt. _____

City   State/Prov.   Zip/Postal Code

Account #_____

Return entry with invoice in reply envelope.

© 1995 HARLEQUIN ENTERPRISES LTD.   CLV KAL

FLYAWAY VACATION
SWEEPSTAKES

OFFICIAL ENTRY COUPON

This entry must be received by: JULY 30, 1995
This month's winner will be notified by: AUGUST 15, 1995
Trip must be taken between: SEPTEMBER 30, 1995-SEPTEMBER 30, 1996

YES, I want to win a vacation for two in Las Vegas. I understand the prize includes round-trip airfare, first-class hotel and $500.00 spending money. Please let me know if I'm the winner!

Name_____

Address _____ Apt. _____

City   State/Prov.   Zip/Postal Code

Account #_____

Return entry with invoice in reply envelope.

© 1995 HARLEQUIN ENTERPRISES LTD.   CLV KAL